STAR TREK: FROM OUTER SPACE TO INNER SPACE

Karin Blair plumbs the depths of STAR TREK and the universal unconscious to explain how—and why—a television series has become a modern myth and an international phenomenon. From the archetypal ENTERPRISE to the aliens within and without, she explores an ancient world brought to the public consciousness in the language of our age: television. It is a look at each and every one of us, the world we have left and the world we have yet to reach.

"I learned much from Karin Blair's book . . . about STAR TREK AND MYSELF. A most unusual and interesting analysis of our television show. I enjoyed it thoroughly."

—Gene Roddenberry

"Karin Blair's account of the sources of the show's success in terms of Jungian archetypes is surprising and convincing . . . excellent . . ."

—Robert Scholes

". . . a very thorough, intelligent and meaningful piece of work . . . it will add much to the body of literature on the subject."

—Leonard Nimoy

Meaning In
STAR TREK

KARIN BLAIR

WARNER BOOKS

A Warner Communications Company

Meaning in Star Trek*

WARNER BOOKS EDITION

*Star Trek is a trademark of Paramount Pictures Corporation, which has no connection with this book.

Library of Congress Catalog Card Number 77-7438

ISBN 0-446-92095-9

This Warner Books Edition is published by arrangement with Anima Books

Cover design by New Studio Inc.

Book design by Helen Roberts

Warner Books, Inc., 75 Rockefeller Plaza, New York, N.Y. 10019

W A Warner Communications Company

Printed in the United States of America

Not associated with Warner Press, Inc. of Anderson, Indiana

First Printing: March, 1979

10 9 8 7 6 5 4 3 2 1

Contents

MEANING IN
STAR TREK

Myth is an act of faith in a science yet unborn.

—*Claude Lévi-Strauss*

Preface

This book is for those who seek to understand the appeal of *Star Trek,* which touches a vast body of fans, unprecedented both in number and in devotion in the history of television. Examining the show involves examining ourselves, for just as it originated in Gene Roddenberry's experiences of alienation as an asthmatic child,[1] so it touches viewers where they feel alien and in need of a more generous concept of self and society in which the alien has a place.

My own life intersects with *Star Trek* both historically and geographically—I have long since felt like an alien in both time and place. My parents were divorced when I was two, before it was fashionable or even acceptable, and my

[1] *Inside Star Trek,* Columbia Records 34279

mother, with whom I lived, kept my father's identity secret until I was into my teens. Considered sickly, I was kept home from school until the second half of the third grade. On my first day at school, I was bombarded with *the* question that comes to those raised in a patriarchal society: Who are you?—that is—Who is your father? Of course, I did not know and could not have felt more like a fatherless and therefore only half-human hybrid from another planet. So it was that I was launched on a long adventure to learn who I was.

The girl without a father has special problems relating to the masculine and what it implies of intellect, authority, and desire. I find in the character of Spock a significant innovation whose relevance to women is evident in the welcome he has received. Analysis of his character can serve as a focal point around which to integrate perceptions and problems dealing with the masculine in various ways. Women frequently alienated from this part of themselves by guilt can identify with him and through him with the world of the *Enterprise*. As the masculine is made available to women, a larger and more positive concept of the feminine can emerge, perhaps with important implications for the self-images available to men as well as women. Spock, as a catalyst for the future, can offer us a new image for integrity and growth.

Alien at home, I went to live in French-speaking Europe with my husband and daughter only to experience alienness abroad. We have been living in Switzerland, a country the size of Lake Michigan, where the line between the foreign and the familiar can fall between towns hardly five miles apart. As Americans, we have had our floors explored by guests curious about alien sanitary practices. Water dripping from my window boxes onto those of the neighbor below has been cursed as if it carried fatal spores or cosmic viruses. I know how Spock's ears feel.

On returning to the States, we were greeted by *Star Trek,* which greatly eased reentry from orbiting Europe. We had been told to expect a country revolutionized by the upheavals of the late 'sixties, the agonies of the Vietnam War, the crises of Watergate. We knew that America, compared to Europe, is the land of change, and we wondered how many generations we had missed. Would we once more be aliens coming from the far side of the line between the foreign and the familiar?

For reasons which are explored throughout the book, the *Star Trek* effect is unifying. As Spock could serve as mediator to parts of myself, so the program could function in relation to my country. Researching the *Star Trek* phenomenon opened doors for us with a speed and warmth which would have been difficult to imagine beforehand. With generosity and kindness, Gene Roddenberry took time to talk with us in December; Leonard Nimoy and D. C. Fontana in January. Not only have we been granted lengthy interviews with busy people, but we have been given scripts, posters, programs, buttons, badges, fanzines, and even tribbles, those space guinea pigs which happily reproduce only on the TV screen.

Having studied folklore, the popular culture

of the past, usually produced anonymously, I was pleasantly surprised when Joan Winston, co-author of *Star Trek Lives!* reminded me that most of the people involved in *Star Trek* are known, alive, and well. John Cawelti of the University of Chicago sent me to Gary Wolfe and Curt Clemmer of Roosevelt University, who shared their enthusiasms and the story of an inspired decision to dress security guards at the Chicago Convention in Klingon costumes, evoking a role-magic that made any aggression a thrilling and photogenic event even for "victims." "Knock me down again, Klingon, so mom can take a picture!" Also in Chicago, Beverly Friend who, through the Science Fiction Research Association (secretary: L. W. Curry, Hand Ave., Elizabethtown, N. Y. 12932) is actively encouraging the study of science fiction in schools, shared her resources with me.

En route for California, we interviewed Gene Roddenberry, who is central to everything to do with *Star Trek*. Not only did he create the essential components of the show and shape the scripts used, but also through the effect of his leadership he generated a unified family feeling among those involved such that everyone's creativity could flourish and contribute to the enterprise. Given a context and a focus by Gene Roddenberry, the many people involved could work together to inspire and be inspired by one another. It is thanks to him that I can write about *Star Trek* as a unified world.

Special thanks also go to Leonard Nimoy, who, although he could easily have publicly ex-

ploited his role as Spock, has insisted on his
personal integrity and thereby left Spock free to
become part of all our imaginations. His secretary, Teresa Victor, and Susan Sackett, the edi-
tor of *Letters to Star Trek*, helped us on our way
in Los Angeles. Writer D. C. Fontana gave us
unique insights into the world of television production. We were also able to meet B. J. O. Trim-
ble and thank her in person for her *Star Trek
Concordance*, which helped greatly in assembling
this book.

Participants in the Star Trek Welcommittee,
particularly Helen Young of Houston, Texas, and
Stephen Clarke of Dayton, Ohio, helped with
leads and information, as did Louise Strange,
president of the Leonard Nimoy Fan Club (4612
Denver Ct., Englewood, Ohio 45322). Dona
Kerns of Los Altos, California, welcomed us into
her home and the world of conventions. Closer
to home, Douglas and Janie Kriner of St. Thomas, Pa., have shared all manner of *Star Trek*
knowledge and experience with us.

Thanks to all these people—plus many
others, amateur and professional, who have com-
mented on the *Star Trek* phenomenon—I need
not write yet another behind-the-scenes look at
Star Trek but can move into an analysis of some
of its underlying structures.

Outside of the *Star Trek* circle several individuals have furthered this project through their
thoughtful readings and comments; among them
are science-fiction scholar Robert Scholes at
Brown University and Swiss psychiatrist Michel
de Syon. Sharon Ghertman, Carolyn Demaree,

and Jay McLeester, associated with Wilson College, offered a helpful diversity of perspective. Andrew Joscelyne, Ivor Indyk, and Richard Waswo, along with Evelyn Juers and Ann Waswo, all friends at the English Department of the University of Geneva, have generously shared good criticism and good conversation.

Raymond A. Ballinger of Philadelphia contributed counsel on design. Rebecca Nisley copyedited the manuscript, which Faye Wilson typed. Thomas Kapacinskas of Notre Dame University arranged for me to try out some of my ideas at the 1977 convention of the C. G. Jung Society held there. Finally, Harry Buck, friend and collaborator, with his wife Esther, has supported my efforts for numerous years in innumerable ways.

Several institutions have also provided me with indispensable assistance. Lincoln Enterprises (P. O. Box 69470, Los Angeles, California 90069) sells scripts, photographs, film clips, costumes, calendars, and other realia. Thanks to the generous donation of Gene Roddenberry, the Theatre Arts Library of the University of California, Los Angeles, has the working scripts of all the *Star Trek* episodes. The library of Wilson College, Chambersburg, Pennsylvania, made available to me secondary source books from all over the East Coast which were essential to developing the context in which I view *Star Trek*.

Given the lack of transporter travel and mind-melding, my husband, Jay, and my daughter, Ann, with whom I have shared many hours of driving, television viewing, talking, fighting, editing, writing, are in every way a part of this book. Together they have counselled and con-soled, criticized and kept the house together in the absence of computerized food synthesizers and robot-repair-persons. The fun we have shared among ourselves and with our friends who wel-comed us home after our inner space flight is well worth a retarded technology.

For us to see what it is to be human,
as opposed to merely male or female,
we need a non-human shadow,
a world other than our own.

Robert Scholes

1 In Celebration of the Alien

In one way or another we are all aliens; alienness
and alienation are essential human experiences
which people have been pondering for centuries.
How one finds and comes to know oneself depends in part on how one perceives the Other,
what one is not. Thus alienness depends on an
imaginary line which separates the known from
the unknown, the familiar from the foreign, the
"I" from the "Other." Within the world of *Star
Trek* the viewer confronts an obvious alien, Mr.
Spock. In addition, each adventure poses another
range of alien presences encountered by the starship *Enterprise*.

Gene Roddenberry, in creating the world of
the *Enterprise,* envisioned a microcosm where
even an alien could find a home. Spock was not

only accepted by the viewing public, he was embraced. During its second year of production in 1967-1968, the show was jokingly called "The Mr. Spock Hour." Spock's presence is essential to fulfilling the mission of the *Enterprise:* to explore new worlds, to contact new life forms, to reach out to the alien. Spock is both an image for the unknown territory of the alien and a mediator between the familiar and the foreign. In *Star Trek,* Roddenberry made a universe where known must be brought into contact with the unknown, where drama is played out on the borderline between self-definition and self-annihilation. The great enterprise at stake is dramatizing our own encounters with the unknown and hence with the alien within ourselves, as well as the alien beyond. It is an evolutionary process like life.

Also, as in life, this process of encountering the unknown involves us with both the familiarity of the past and the foreignness of the future. One of the paradoxes encountered in any attempt to move beyond the known is that the human mind can make contact only with that which is already in some way familiar. Therefore an alien, to be comprehensible, must also have some familiar characteristics. Spock the hybrid Vulcan-human can function as resident alien precisely because he is *half* human and can therefore dramatize the point of contact between the familiar and the foreign. Spock's foreignness, on the other hand, allows us to see—worked out in him and hence in ourselves—the relation between polarities usually seen as diametrically opposed in our human world. Just as Vulcans rarely marry humans, so intellect rarely mates easily with emotion, and moral goodness seems incompatible with overwhelming mating urges. Such oppositions between mind and body are bridged in the character of Spock who, offspring of a Vulcan father and a Terran mother, must continually overcome in himself the tension between mind and emotion, moral dedication to Kirk and the sexual heat of *pon farr*[1] under the influence of which he could kill his captain. Such tensions in Spock are dramatized on a larger scale in the encounters of the *Enterprise* with still more alien beings. Although familiar polarities establish the terms of the problems Spock and the *Enterprise* must cope with, they do not circumscribe the final outcome. Instead the dynamic tension between opposing forces animates both the characters and the episodes. The psyche of the viewer is stimulated in its own evolution by encountering these old polarities newly combined first of all in Spock, then in the voyages of the starship, then in ourselves.

In the world of *Star Trek*, certain polarities are especially prominent: good and evil, female and male, young and old. In human society, cultural codes function to maintain more or less clear distinctions between such categories. However assiduously a person tries to fit the main cultural categories of the surroundings, she/he will one day find within her/himself elements that do

1. *Pon farr* refers to the Vulcan mating urge which once every seven years overwhelms the male to the extent that he must return home and submit to the Vulcan rituals surrounding it or die. The dramatic situation in the episode *Amok Time* centers on *pon farr* and was created in response to viewer interest in the character of Spock. (See below, Chapter 4, pp. 62–82.)

not fit. These elements are immediately seen as undesirable and alienating, yet at the same time they provide the stimulus toward what Arthur Miller has identified as the theme of all worthwhile drama: a person's search to make a home in the outside world. The challenge is to make a world in which we can come to terms with rejected parts of ourselves—in short, to feel at home both within ourselves and in the world around us. Perhaps from this perspective we can approach an understanding of the unprecedented appeal of *Star Trek* to the television viewing public.

Here is a world where tension is no longer moralized as guilt but universalized as energy; difference is not condemned but embraced as *IDIC*: infinite diversity in infinite combinations. Life is celebrated even at the expense of peace and moral self-righteousness. The world of *Star Trek* is structured out of polarities no longer condemned for dividing some ideally unitary world but embraced for providing energy and direction for future evolution. Growth, not guilt, becomes the fruit of alienation, just as renewal rather than shame can be the result of sexual union. Home can be found not in some unrecoverable past but in the process of discovery.

The Impact of Star Trek

Although cancelled in 1969 and slated for a quiet demise as a rerun, *Star Trek* has attracted a fan following that is unique in the history of television. Overwhelming attraction, as in *pon farr*, is not always intellectually predictable.

In 1964, Gene Roddenberry began working on *Star Trek* and by 1966 the first year of production was under way. Twenty-six new episodes were filmed each season for three years. In the latter part of this period, ratings based on the viewing preferences of the sampling of "typical" American families indicated that the program was not drawing the eighteen million viewers per broadcast hour then needed to justify continuation. Production on new episodes stopped, and the show could be seen only on reruns. At this moment, professionals in the entertainment field, including even Gene Roddenberry, saw the show as entertainment which would fade into obscurity. It was only after *Star Trek* conventions began to flourish in 1971-1972, that they realized they had misjudged the program's impact. Demographic analysis of the viewing public verified earlier misjudgments; statistics revealed that in fact *Star Trek's* viewing profile had just the concentration of young couples and the soon-to-be-married that advertisers sought. Since then the show's popularity has been growing in steady progression. Although science fiction has always attracted a distinctive following, *Star Trek* fans have distinguished themselves through their number and diversity and through the intensity of their commitment. More than a million fan letters have been responsible for keeping the show on the air, first in 1968, then in reruns; some 400,000 fan letters convinced then President Ford to name the first American space shuttlecraft the *Enterprise,* a name which retains its meaning in several languages. *Star Trek* conventions continue all over the country and are frequently the scene of ritual repetition of *Star Trek* scripts by fans who have memorized all the lines.

The *Star Trek* phenomenon is unique, not only in its intensity, but also in its breadth. Some 140 domestic stations broadcast the show on more or less continuous rerun; 115 foreign stations have also broadcast it, either in translation or with subtitles.[2] *Star Trek* crosses national boundaries with the ease of light. The appeal of the show leaps temporal boundaries just as easily as it does national ones. There are more fans today than ever before, and among them are some who were not even born when the program began. Although the youth of many viewers is implicit in the *Star Trek* gadgetry which is aimed at them, there are Golden Age fan clubs for trekkies among the retired. Just as *Star Trek's* appeal cuts across the boundaries of age and nationality, so also it defies easy categorization by other means. The product of Hollywood in the late 1960s, *Star Trek* generates a force field which extends far beyond its origins.

The impact of this force field on viewers has been as various as the individuals involved. *Letters to Star Trek* reports that autistic children have been able to direct their energies outward in attempts to draw or talk about Spock. Adults have moved across the country and changed their professions to be involved in the world of *Star Trek*. Since we are dealing with science fiction, where futuristic technology provides the framework within which the drama occurs, some viewers feel that the program really prefigures a possi-

2. Susan Sackett, ed., *Letters to Star Trek* (New York: Ballantine, 1977).

ble future for the world and have set about to implement comparable advances in society.

As *The Making of Star Trek*[3] makes clear, the show takes great care to maintain scientific plausibility; Roddenberry and his production staff consulted research institutes to assure the verisimilitude essential to establishing scientific credibility. Nonetheless, scientific interest cannot circumscribe its world even for its fans, nor can it account for the intensity of their interest. The promise of being examined on a bed modelled after those in the sick bay of the *Enterprise* (and such apparently do exist) is not enough to motivate the memorization of scripts. Nor is the scientific verisimilitude uniform throughout the show. Shock waves from explosions continue to rock the *Enterprise* for dramatic reasons even though they cannot actually exist in the virtual vacuum of outer space. In addition, the final outcome of episodes only rarely turn on scientific details of warp drive, time travel, or transporter functioning taken for their own sakes. Even when, for example, in *The Enterprise Incident,* the plot's resolution depends on the successful utilization of the captured Romulan cloaking device, there is no elaboration of the technology involved. This piece of Romulan hardware which endows its user with invisibility serves itself as a cloaking device for the core of the show's interest: the relationship between Spock and the beautiful Romulan commander.

Another factor controlling the importance of space technology is the "Prime Directive"

3. Stephen Whitfield and Gene Roddenberry, *The Making of Star Trek* (New York: Ballantine, 1968).

which forbids interference with the evolution of an alien society. In *The Enterprise Incident* the drama is between technological equals: the Romulans and the United Federation of Planets; therefore, the Prime Directive does not apply. Very often, however, the starship encounters less advanced societies and hence must restrain its technology. Space hardware is thereby placed in a moral framework. The question of whose control panel triggers the most powerful display of technology is never by itself the controlling factor.

Over the years several other explanations of the popularity of *Star Trek* have been proposed. Some have attributed the show's appeal to its play of ideas. Yet although it is popular with university audiences, its fans cannot be categorized as only intellectuals. As Gene Roddenberry explained in an interview, the show also has an audience in institutions for the mentally retarded. While various episodes do deal intellectually with most of today's pressing problems such as war, prejudice, and mechanization, for example, there must be something in the presentation which transcends ideas and can speak to viewers with lesser as well as greater mental ability.

Star Trek appeals not only to the emotionally stable but also to the disturbed: the episode entitled *The Enemy Within*, in particular, has been used as an unusually effective psychotherapeutic teaching device. In this episode Kirk, the captain of the starship, is accidentally split into two persons, one of whom, the positive Kirk, self-effacing and kind, is at odds with negative Kirk, who is anti-social and savage—his concerns are alcohol, sex, and aggression. As the plot unfolds, we see the positive Kirk becoming forgetful, indecisive, and generally unable to command; we see that he needs his negative self, which is now dying from general psychosomatic imbalance. Resolution comes once positive Kirk controls the repulsion he feels for his aggressive half and embraces his anti-social self so that, reunited, the whole Kirk can live. In short, we need both halves of ourselves even if one part seems undesirable and evil. Aggression is essential for a successful captain and an integrated human being.

Those who prefer an emotional explanation for the show's appeal invoke "love." The fan authors of *Star Trek Lives!* are the most vocal proponents of this theory, verbalizing what the majority of viewers surely senses: that there is a notable *esprit de corps* among the actors who mutually enjoyed working with one another. Gene Roddenberry himself acknowledges not only that the *Star Trek* cast formed an unusually cohesive group, but that such an outcome had in fact been one of his initial aims. Producing the series was for him not only an artistic and intellectual challenge, but a human one as well. He wanted to create a family feeling on both the *Enterprise* and Paramount's back lot. His success is evident, not only in what script writer D. C. Fontana describes as an absence of Hollywood "claim jumping," but in the presence of mutual appreciation of what each person could contribute to the show.

An interesting example of crew participation emerged when a prop man with a special talent for monsters, James Prohaska, who was working on the same lot as the *Star Trek* crew, made a large lumpy, rock monster and demonstrated it for Gene Roddenberry, who in turn liked the creature so much that he asked his collaborator, the late Gene Coon, to write a script for it. Thus was born the horta, and it went on to inhabit one of the most popular episodes, *The Devil in the Dark.*

The central importance of Gene Roddenberry in all dimensions of the show is hard to overemphasize. As creator of the series, he generated characters which were initially parts of himself, as we shall see further in Chapter 10. In addition, although the scripts were credited to specific writers with differing styles and ideas, each one was subjected to Gene Roddenberry's scrutiny and revision during the first two years, and thereafter those who had already worked with him carried on. Also, partly as a result of the supportive atmosphere he created among the crew, the characters continued to develop through the commitment the actors made to them. The actors, and especially Leonard Nimoy, felt personally involved in maintaining integrity of character, even despite the occasionally insensitive writer or director. In short, the community on the bridge of the *Enterprise* was nourished by the continued close cooperation of its creators.

The Alien Within

Such unity on the technological, intellectual, and human levels leads one toward an explanation of *Star Trek's* appeal based on more universal factors. A broadly gauged psychological approach can allow us to see how production staff as well as viewers could be turned on to this enterprise. On the screen and behind the scenes alike, the televised and human drama creates a context where even the alien, including the alien in us all, could feel at home. The "I" and the potentially threatening "Other" need no longer be doomed to perpetual and fearful opposition.

This unknown and often threatening alien that we each have within ourselves translates into psychological terms as the *unconscious mind,* that part of ourselves which we by definition do not know and, in some cases, do not want to recognize. As we saw in *The Enemy Within,* Kirk's "other half" emerges as essential to the integrity of the captain. Kirk's temptation to claim-jump by rejecting the right of this alien to an appropriate place within his personal being is countered by Spock, the resident alien who must live with his own duality. He convinces the captain that both halves are necessary to successfully carry on function and being.

In *The Enemy Within,* we see the alien as unconsciousness in fairly traditional Freudian terms: the repressed forces of aggression and sexuality. Carl Gustav Jung, the Swiss founder of analytical psychology, distinguished himself from his mentor, Sigmund Freud, the founder of psychoanalysis, by enlarging the idea of the unconscious. To Jung, the unconscious includes not only what one does not want to know, repressed feelings of aggression and rejection based on personal childhood experiences, but also what one *cannot* know. The transcendent as well as the rejected part of human experience is part of the unconscious. Dreams as well as works of art and other creations of the imagination such as myth and even mathematics offer glimpses of this other world. Having studied the products of the human mind and imagination from many cultures, Jung felt he had found recurrent patterns. For example, human beings in many times and places have found importance in myths having similar structures. On the basis of his findings he elaborated a theory of archetypal psychology.

Psychic health depends on a living relationship with the unconscious. The healthy psyche must always be a function of *both* of its two components: the *immanent* world of one's individual consciousness and the *transcendent* world lying beyond the frontiers of one's knowledge.[4] What makes the connection Jung calls *archetypes*?

Archetypes as Jung understands them are "empty and purely formal,"[5] that is, they are analogous to the "axial system of a crystal, which as it were, performs the crystalline structure in the mother liquid, although it has no material existence of its own."[6] Since every crystal of the same compound always takes the same shape, we conceive of the axial system as independent of any particular crystal, thereby constituting a series of rules or structures which becomes visible only after the crystal is formed. Similarly, for Jung, "A primordial [archetypal] image is determined as to its content only when it has become conscious and therefore filled out with the ma-

---

4. Carl Gustav Jung, *Collected Works* (Princeton: Princeton University Press, Bollingen Series XX, 1953–1976).
5. Jung, 10:410.
6. Jung, 9(1):79.

terial of conscious experience."[7] The content of an archetype, then, reflects individual and cultural experience which is subject to change, whereas its form reflects basic psychic structures.

Thus a basic archetypal structure must be fleshed out and made visible by a succession of different contents which have living resonance in different times and places. The danger for Jungians is to mistake the content of a particular manifestation of an archetype ("the Demeter archetype," "the Eden archetype") for the underlying pattern which manifests itself again and again in human experience. Cultural experience is subject to change, however slowly, with the result that the living archetypes of an earlier era survive only a dead mythology which no longer commands belief or offers the medium for living contact between the unconscious and conscious worlds in the psyche. The archetype is an activity by which we can relate the conscious to the unconscious. The particular stories and images that can reactivate and make comprehensible the primordial psychic structures must be created anew again and again if they are to galvanize the energies of psychic health.

The function of archetypes then is to mediate between the realms of the conscious and the unconscious, and the archetype *par excellence* is Number. "Between them stands the great mediator, Number, whose reality is valid in both worlds, an archetype in its very essence." We are all familiar with the conscious and practical significance of number as a way of counting. As Jung

7. Jung, 10:409.

points out, however, ". . . numbers . . . this side of the border are quantities but on the other are autonomous psychic entities, capable of making qualitative statements . . ."[8] In short, number bridges the familiar polarities of the quantitative versus the qualitative, intellect versus emotion, conscious versus unconscious.

For a specific example, the number *one* has two dimensions with which everyone is familiar. In addition to its quantitative aspect, it has qualitative resonance with *oneness*. The latter has traditionally been associated with the cultural stereotype of Eden and has been interestingly adapted and modified in the *Star Trek* episode entitled *The Way to Eden*. The oneness of traditional Eden has been transformed in the *Star Trek* context: an image that for centuries retained its psychological impact as a symbol for unconscious unity is seen in the episode as culture-bound and outmoded.

From Stereotype to Archetype: *The Way to Eden*

In *The Way to Eden* we see a group of space hippies try to realize their dream of a return to our cultural prototype of paradise. Having stolen a space cruiser, they are apprehended by the *Enterprise* and taken aboard. Their anarchic ways anger Kirk, who as captain represents the military hierarchy of the Federation. Their somewhat bizarre unisex clothing further sets them apart from the rest of the crew, as does their focus on

8. Jung, 10:409-11.

play rather than work. Spock, however, is able to establish rapport with them, first of all by means of the circular hand sign signifying oneness with which they greet one another. On further contact, they discover and appreciate Spock's musical ability and find in him someone with whom they can play. Furthermore, whereas Kirk dismisses Eden as a nonexistent myth, Spock is willing to search out its possible reality. For the hippies, Eden is the goal of their search for the oneness of unconscious union with a fertile, bountiful, and all-embracing Mother Nature. Spock, appropriately for the resident alien on the *Enterprise,* feels sympathy for these young people who disobey the accepted working rules of society. By putting his research skills to work he discovers that there *is* a planet called Eden.

The outcome of the episode depends on Spock as mediator first of all between their ideal goal and the planet which the *Enterprise* visits. Eden, when subjected to actual investigation, is revealed to be quite other than the fabulous garden. Although on first appearance it lives up to its model—lush greenery bearing abundant fruit—on closer contact the hippies discover that the sap of the vegetation is in fact a harmful acid. They cannot leave their shuttlecraft without burning their feet, and, as the leader, Sevrin, demonstrates, to eat the fruit is fatal. The Eden where there is no labor, competition, or need for order, no self-consciousness or responsibility, only appears attractive; in actuality, it proves uninhabitable.

"Paradise" comes from the Persian word *pairidaeza,* meaning not "garden" but "wall" or "enclosure." From there it made its way into the Bible as garden or orchard. As we see the final shots of the hippies huddled together within the confines of a shuttlecraft, we are invited to see that the paradise they sought is an enclosure constructed by the human mind, just as is the circle. Their dream of an undifferentiated unity without walls or distinctions is an idealization of unconsciousness and perhaps ultimately of death.

Such an idealized notion of Eden can no longer mediate between the conscious and unconscious mind, conceived as it is so exclusively in terms of unconsciousness. Thus this idealized Eden, one example of what Jungians would call the "paradise archetype," has in fact lost its archetypal function. In our time it no longer mediates but rather reiterates cultural values in stereotyped form. As such it functions to differentiate those who believe in it from the "others"; thus in human terms it alienates rather than integrates. On the other hand, Spock, by using the circular hand sign, was not expressing a value but affirming a symbolic context within which his world can coexist with that of the hippies. The unity shared by Spock and the hippies was not based on intellectual agreement or moral judgment or even shared emotional state; rather it came from within the structure of the psyche and was based on currents and forces that are part of every human being regardless of time, place, or emotional state. Thus, through Spock, the circle could retain an archetypal function by relating a stereotype—Eden—with contemporary consciousness. In this perspective, *Star Trek* represents as much of an innovation as does Spock. It has taken historically and psychically opposed forces and placed them in a new relationship to each other. Whereas death awaits one on the planet Eden, the tree of life grows within a walled garden, and life goes on inside the walls of the *Enterprise,* within the structures of the human psyche.

Our world has shrunk,
and it is dawning on us that humanity is *one*,
with one psyche.

C. G. Jung

2 The Archetypal Enterprise

The Starship *Enterprise* is composed of a circle and three cigar-shapes. The very simplicity of these shapes is important and contributes to the universal or archetypal resonance of the *Enterprise,* which is not shared, for example, by the space eagles in the television series *Space 1999* or the various airborne objects we see on the screen of *UFO*. Although Gene Roddenberry did not intellectualize his reasons, he spent a good deal of time and effort on the shape of the starship, waching it evolve through many stages until it finally "felt right." Let's look at some of the implications of his choice of forms.

Circle as Mandala

Unity or totality has in nearly all times and places been symbolized by the circle. In the East, the circle as symbol is most often stylized as the lotus flower; in the West we often find Christ at the center of a circle with the four evangelists at the cardinal points of the compass; in North America the traditional sand paintings of the Pueblo and Navajo Indians often constellate around the circle. Jung found that the circle was often produced in patients' drawings; sometimes they even danced circles in sessions devoted to free self-expression. Although ignorant of the meaning of the circle, the patients were "fascinated by them and [found] that they somehow [expressed] and [had] an effect on their subjective psychic state."[1] Such metaphysical circles are called *mandalas,* which is Sanskrit for "magic circle."

The magic of the circle as a mathematical perfection may in fact have retarded its entry into the world of number and practicality. Although the circular is everywhere in nature—in the sun and the moon, the iris of the eye, the eggs of animals and the fruits of plants—the wheel for a long time was not a universal tool. The religion of the Incas, for example, permitted the reproduction of circles only as sun wheels or wheels on children's toys. They did not put the circle-as-wheel to practical use since in their minds it was a sacred symbol of the sun. Children might play with circles, but adults must worship them.

1. Jung, 13:23.

Similarly, in the field of number, zero is a late comer. Less than two thousand years ago, theorists in India integrated it into mathematics and evolved the decimal system, which was transmitted to the West by the Arabs to become the basis of modern computation. Originally the concept of zero was part of the Indian metaphysical system where it symbolized infinity. As Coomaraswamy says,

> to the Indian mind all numbers are virtually or potentially present in that which is without number, . . . [thus] zero is to number as potentiality is to actuality.[2]

Thus zero began its career as symbol of unity, as undifferentiated potentiality from which all life flows. It is nothing and yet potentially everything.

Today we cannot imagine life without the wheel or the zero, which because of its use in the binary language of the computer has assumed great importance along with the number one. We live at the end of a long process of secularization and now the circle is an everyday helper. When we encounter it as the structuring principle of the *Enterprises's* bridge, this trajectory of history is reversed. This circle is not primarily a practical principle of organization; rather it carries a symbolic meaning important for its impact on the psyche. That "something special" which we find

2. A. K. Coomaraswamy, "Kha and Other Words Denoting Zero in Connection With the Metaphysics of Space," *Bulletin of the School of Oriental Studies*, London Institution, Part 3, 1934, p. 496, as quoted in Joanna Macy, "Perfection of Wisdom: Mother of All Buddhas," *Anima*, III/1:1977.

on the bridge of the *Enterprise* makes it not only a stage but a symbol whose shape speaks to us all.

The Bridge as Mandala

The symbolism of the bridge of the *Enterprise* is reinforced with each episode that opens and closes there. This magic circle of wholeness is drawn around the crew as they move freely through space. The adventure begins when encounters with alien presences disrupt their movement and break open the containment of the bridge—someone beams down, someone is beamed aboard, the shuttlecraft must be used. The *Enterprise* must interrupt its trajectory and, in keeping with its mission to go where no man has gone before, follow the thread of an episode's challenge. From the balance of the bridge the crew must go out to encounter the forces of imbalance or opposition. Their successful resolution is symbolized by a return to the bridge and the mission to seek out knowledge of the unknown. The plot of most episodes is circular insofar as each begins in and returns to the harmony of the bridge. Whereas movement suggests quest, closure indicates completeness.

Kirk as Focal Point

Kirk, at the center of this circular microcosm, sets up a differentiation essential for human functioning. The unknown can be approached only through its contrastive relation to the known. In fact, we humans often come to know an entity by defining its relation to its polar opposite. Hence familiar polarities: masculine and feminine, good and evil, youth and age. Although perhaps at times the potential for conflict in polarities seems undesirable, it is a condition of knowledge and consciousness. As Jung points out, "The one universal being cannot be known, because it is not differentiated from anything and cannot be compared with anything."[3] As long as a thing remains unconscious, it has no recognizable qualities and is indistinguishable from anything else. It emerges into existence only insofar as we separate it from what it is *not* by means of the four basic psychic faculties we are endowed with. It can be (1) perceived by the senses (Spock picks up an unknown object on a sensor scan), or (2) analyzed by the intellect (Spock correlates the data and explains the most logical means of approach), or (3) evaluated by the feelings (McCoy exclaims that one can't do that!), or (4) grasped in its implications by the intuition (McCoy protests that a certain action might mean the destruction of the ship). These four faculties can be understood as two pairs of polar opposites: two ways of perceiving the world, sensation (2) and intuition (4); and two ways of digesting these perceptions, intellect (1) and its opposite, emotion (3); Kirk at the center of the bridge is symbolically surrounded by four crew members—navigator, helmsman, science officer, and communications officer—who provide the data necessary to make informed judgments and implement his commands.

At the center of the bridge, Kirk is thus at the center of opposing ways of dealing with the

3. Jung, 10:407.

world, ways which are embodied, for example, in Spock, the science officer, and McCoy, the physician. The position of his chair repeats his centrality as captain in relation to the crew on the bridge. In addition he provides the central point of union between his two chief consultants and friends, Spock and McCoy. To be a *mandala*, a circle needs a center through which consciousness and unconsciousness are united. Kirk is the center of such a circle whose circumference always includes Spock, the alien. An analysis of the characters of Kirk, Spock, and McCoy will follow; for the moment a brief look at the command center of Moonbase Alpha on *Space 1999* will provide a helpful comparison.

Star Trek versus Space 1999

The television series *Space 1999* takes place on Earth's moon, adrift in space with no purpose other than survival. The command center, science laboratory, and sick bay have no visual relation to one another, nor to the spherical shape of the moon. In the command center, the two banks of desks with instruments face a viewing screen. Their arrangement suggests a grade-school classroom presided over by a benevolent father-figure. Nothing, moreover, in the commander's character or position probes what it is that makes one a captain of oneself or others. Just as there is no direction to the moon's trajectory, so there is neither directional organization of internal space nor implied human relationships capable of archetypal resonance.

Kirk, on the other hand, sits at the center of

the starship, of the bridge, of himself. He is a focal point. He receives information from the officers with access to the bridge, including the opposing perspectives of Spock and McCoy, i.e., from all four faculties. As captain, he transforms the information into decision and action; from him as center radiates a new circle of conscious activity in relation to which the *Enterprise* itself becomes a circular, containing, feminine entity, a vehicle for successfully encountering the unknown. To Kirk, as a man, the *Enterprise,* his ship, is his woman.

Circle as Feminine Symbol

As Kirk says in *Metamorphosis,* gender differentiation is universal. Like the circle, sexuality is a principle known to people of all times and places. Perhaps because all people are born of mothers, the feminine has long been associated with the unconsciousness from which the infant is ejected at birth, leaving consciousness to characterize its generic opposite, the masculine. As the individual begins to distinguish him/herself as a being distinct from the mother, consciousness becomes identified as masculine. With this conscious pole are associated clarity in contrast to mystery, light rather than darkness, pursuit as opposed to receptivity, discrimination versus acceptance, culture rather than nature, a series to which one could add hierarchy as opposed to anarchy, work rather than play, and many others.

When Kirk in *The Corbomite Maneuver* says to McCoy that the *Enterprise* is his woman, he is repeating a division of the world as old and universal as the circle. To the Chinese there was the *yang* or the masculine principle and the *yin*, the feminine. In India the *lingam* and the *yoni*, the phallus and the vulva, similarly symbolized the essential forces in the cosmos. Some of the oldest human artifacts are stone representations of the phallus and the vulva, whence the straight and the circular ritual object, the one and the zero of the computer. These same structures resurface in dreams and other products of the imagination.

Jung had a number of patients in whose dreams various UFOs appeared. A healing sequence of such dreams often involved a feminine round shape balanced with a cigar-shaped masculine complement. The imagination of the creative artist similarly works within the limits of the psyche itself and thus often within the structure of the balance of opposites reflected in the round and the straight. In this perspective, it is no surprise that the *Enterprise* is the most widely sold model spacecraft in history. Embodying simple and archetypal forms, the circular and the linear, it has universal resonance. In comparison, the bug-eyed insect shapes that often populate science fiction films seem idiosyncratic. In the world of *Star Trek,* however, these traditional oppositions relate to each other in new ways. As we saw in *The Way to Eden,* the representation of the circle as Mother Nature, as Eden, as the natural nurturing feminine is replaced by the circle as the enclosure of the *Enterprise.*

The round body of the starship assumes a feminine character, first in relation to the crew which it carries and cares for, and then in opposition to the three phallic, cigar-shaped engineering and propulsion units. Viewed from above, the round body of the starship resembles a wheel with twenty subdivisions, at the center of which is a light much like the luminous eye found at the center of *mandalas* throughout the world. Viewed from the inside, this central portion constellates around Kirk, figure for the ship's commanding consciousness. As Kirk determines the direction of the starship, so the propulsion units provide the momentum as engagement of matter with antimatter releases energy for motion. However, part of the energy released, like part of the conscious activity on board, goes into the providing, feminine functions of support and sustenance, for example, the computerized food synthesizers and the atmospheric control systems. In short, just as the geometrically perfect *mandala* circle is a structure of the psyche, so the feminine as an idea becomes in the starship articulated into machines created by human consciousness and therefore hierarchy, order, work, intention, decision. *Star Trek* thus turns away from outworn notions of the feminine as unconscious and edenic to a forward-looking embodiment of the feminine within what humans can consciously understand and construct.

From Orbit to Action

While the circle has traditionally implied the stasis of wholeness, the circle of the starship follows a linear trajectory which opens to the unknown and to change. Traditional luminous celestial circles—suns, moons, stars, planets—

follow fixed and circular orbits, while the *Enterprise* moves freely in response to the decisions of its captain and the demands of its mission to explore and increase the range of human consciousness.

The traditional balance between the oppositions of masculine and feminine implicit in the circular and the linear shapes of the *Enterprise* has been modified in the universe of *Star Trek*. Whereas in the dreams of Jung's patients the circular and the linear appeared in balanced sequence, to be united perhaps in the psyche of the dreamer, here they are already united and in motion. In terms of this new union, the *Enterprise* becomes a "masculine" light of consciousness perpetually exploring the dark and mysterious unknown of outer space. The feminine character of this realm is evident in Gene Roddenberry's poem which was originally intended to accompany the musical theme of the show. In it he invokes the "Strange love a star woman teaches" as the goal of a never-ending trek through a space that is beyond even the "rim of . . . star light."[4] The purely "feminine," like pure nature or pure unconsciousness, is ultimately unknowable, as it always has been. What has changed is the locus of symbolic representations of these phenomena. The vision of atonement, of the Heavenly City or the Paradisal Garden, is no longer projected in terms of unconscious union but is recreated within the realm of consciousness. Within the archetypal world of the *Enterprise*, we have a new paradigm for psychic at-

4. Whitfield and Roddenberry, p. 7.

one-ment: the organic harmony of the Garden has been transferred to a world of human creation.

The Garden in the Machine

In *The Machine in the Garden,* Leo Marx explores the pastoral ideal which has defined the meaning of America since its discovery. Confronted with a virgin continent, the Europeans projected on America their dream of natural harmony and joy. The emergence of the machine into this garden, however, shatters the dream and destroys the American hero who has been in pursuit of it. "In the end, he . . . is either dead or totally alienated from society, alone and powerless, like the evicted shepherd of Virgil's eco-logue."[5]

Star Trek has reversed these evaluations, as the episode *The Paradise Syndrome* shows. Kirk, Spock, and McCoy beam down to an idyllic earth-like planet inhabited by American Indians having no trace of technology beyond an obelisk associated with their worship. The mission of the crew of the *Enterprise* is to divert an asteroid which is on a collision course with the planet. In the course of their explorations, Kirk accidentally falls into the obelisk, where an electrical current erases his memory. As he emerges, having recovered his consciousness but not his memory, he is seen by the tribe's priestess who takes him to her father. According to tribal lore he who emerges from the obelisk is considered to be a

5. Leo Marx, *The Machine in the Garden* (New York: Oxford University Press, 1964), p. 364.

demi-god, come to save the tribe from destruction. Kirk, without his memory, assumes the role, which includes taking the priestess as his wife. Here we see enacted the values implicit in the dream of natural joy and harmony. Kirk, happily married, indulges in child-like play in the paradisal setting of virgin nature. His wife also carries his child, a symbol of their union. Similarly, however, his nightly dreams vaguely evoking the *Enterprise* remind the viewer of the loss of memory, which is also essential to their union. If the feminine values of unconscious union, loss of self in the other, submission to an all-providing nature present one aspect of "the paradise syndrome," inflation of self toward the "all" represents another. We see Kirk as the unwilling demigod, Kirok, standing on the obelisk trying to command the powers of nature, which implies the sense of union he wants to feel with them as well. The episode is resolved by Spock, who, having worked continuously night and day to decipher the hieroglyphs, can unlock their code and release the mechanism which will deflect the asteroid. Kirk's wife, Miramanee, dies, taking along with her their unborn child; Kirk, however, is restored to himself through the intermediary of Spock and, joined by McCoy, they beam aboard the *Enterprise*.

In the *Enterprise* itself they rejoin a machine already well above the paradisal garden it has saved from natural destruction. Spock's mental powers are not simply natural, but more particularly, the result of Vulcan training, functioning in conjunction with the ship's computers. On board the *Enterprise* all aspects of life are circumscribed by the technology without which life would cease to exist in outer space. Similarly, everyone on board works to guarantee the continued functioning of the starship. There is a captain at the helm and a mission to accomplish. The sought-after garden is no longer "out there" in nature but inside the human mind and its constructions. The harmony and joy romantics seek in unconscious nature emerge as new human possibilities through cultivation of consciousness. The machine is no longer an engine of opposition, war, and destruction; it has become a vehicle which both nurtures and expresses the human consciousness which created it. Technology has replaced magic; movement has replaced stasis. Within the *Enterprise,* traditionally opposing forces can recombine and generate not only physical motion but human drama. The archetypal qualities of the starship are only a prelude to the psychological relationships which unite the three principal characters, Kirk, Spock, and McCoy. Together these three figures form one family, if not one personality, and provide both continuity from episode to episode and dramatic tension within a given program. They must include the polarities which are the inevitable result of individual consciousness and differentiation and which at times produce conflict. In addition, they give us the means by which our heritage from the past can evolve into greater consciousness in the present and open into visions of the future.

Then, the memories and the
mouths of ancient elders was
the only way that early histor-
ies ... got passed along ...
for all of us today to know
who we are.

Alex Haley

3 McCoy: Distillation
of the Past

We have seen Kirk at the center of the *Enterprise*,
where information is transformed into action.
Just as he is the center of the spatial organization
of the bridge, the link between the starship and
its trajectory, so he represents the interface between the known and the unknown, the past and
the future. On either side of him psychologically
and often physically are his two chief officers:
McCoy and Spock.

Whereas Spock belongs on the bridge as
science officer and second-in-command in the
official hierarchy, McCoy belongs in sick bay as
the physician, who by definition is outside the
chain of authority. Just as Kirk's central position
tells us about his personality as well as about his
function as captain, so McCoy's situation is also

significant. Being outside the chain of command frees him from problems of strategy and other command responsibilities. In *The Tholian Web*, when Kirk is absent, it is Spock who must assume command, not McCoy. In the same episode Spock assembles the crew in the chapel to announce Kirk's apparent loss, thereby functioning as a priest might. Spock admits McCoy to the service only reluctantly, since the doctor's immediate job is to find an antidote. McCoy is not called upon for ritual matters; his duty is to maintain the health of the body and feelings.

And the Children Shall Lead makes this dramatically clear. Once Kirk has placed the orphaned children in the doctor's care, McCoy continues to show concern for their well-being even when they place the rest of the crew in jeopardy. Since he is safely outside the power structure the children wish to take over, he is not subjected to seeing his own inner fears projected visibly before him. Hence he seems to us free of the others' fears of aging, gibberish, or aggression; his inner feelings seem uncomplicated and directed to caring for others. When the final solution does emerge, and the children understand how they have been used by an evil man seeking power, McCoy defines the health or wholeness which is restored to them and to the ship as well in terms of emotion: the children at last can cry over the loss of their parents and be restored to emotional balance.

Being outside the chain of command has other advantages for McCoy because the chief medical officer has access to the ear of the captain to an extent that would be impossible for a junior line officer. Hence, McCoy can make the captain aware of the emotional impact of command decisions and the emotional needs of the crew and its members. In *The Corbomite Manoeuver* McCoy criticizes Kirk for his treatment of a young crewman named Bailey. Kirk had imposed yet another drill on a tired crew only to be exposed to a *real* emergency. Under the accumulated stress of the drills plus that of confronting an outer-space father figure threatening destruction to the entire ship, Bailey cracks. McCoy turns on Kirk for having put Bailey under excessive strain through too rapid promotion to responsibility on the bridge. Whereas Kirk's focus is on the functioning of the *Enterprise,* McCoy's is on the physical and emotional states of the crew members, who to him are all of equal importance.

The captain, of course, is also a member of the crew who is potentially subject to the medical officer's evaluations and judgments. In the process of talking with Kirk, McCoy often allows us to perceive sides of the captain which are not part of his public presentation of self. In *Balance of Terror,* for example, Kirk reveals his inner doubts through dialogue with McCoy. In *The Corbomite Manoeuver,* McCoy cannot resist following his medical examination of Kirk with comments on the captain's relationship with women. And in *Day of the Dove,* McCoy calls Spock and Kirk fools for refusing to fight and engage the obviously evil Klingons in a battle to the death. Who but McCoy could get away with that! Or want that!

McCoy as General Practitioner

McCoy brings to space the once-familiar general practitioner, the good, old-fashioned doctor who takes care of patients when, for whatever reasons, they cannot take care of themselves. He is not the coolly analytical specialist, but like the earlier prototype, is concerned with what is traditionally known as the "whole" person, including both body and feeling. Treatment, in fact, sometimes involves both: Kirk recalls being told by McCoy that a bit of suffering is good for the soul. In *The Deadly Years,* the doctor clearly relishes telling Spock that the shot prepared for him is especially strong, because of his Vulcan nature, *and* painful. He moves beyond Ben Casey or Dr. Kildare to recall a figure from the Middle Ages, the Good Physician, in whose hands suffering is medicinal, emotion a purgative.

Going further back than the Middle Ages, McCoy recalls the Good Samaritan who reminds us that it is good to help humans whatever their situation or state of development. In his hands, the ideal of his profession embodies our Judeo-Christian heritage of charitable service and humanitarianism. In *Mirror, Mirror* he cannot leave his wounded antagonist, bearded Spock II, even at the risk of being unable to return to the *Enterprise.* In *Bread and Circuses* he says explicitly that just once he would like to be seen as an archangel beaming down from the heavens, a mental scenario obviously spoiled by the presence of the pointed-eared Spock.

His humanitarianism leads him sometimes

into the folksy, for example when he says that good food and plenty of exercise are still the best guarantees of health, or that rest and liquids are the best remedy for the common cold (*The Omega Glory*), or that he still puts his trust in a good pair of tonsils (*The Man Trap*). Sometimes it leads him further into a kind of old womanish fussiness with scientific techniques. He dislikes the transporter, for example: he does not think that human beings should be taken apart and put back together nor does he want his molecules scrambled. In *Spectre of the Gun* he fumes about a possible transporter malfunction when they discover that the planet is not as their sensor scan had predicted. While Spock computes a possible explanation, McCoy complains.

Even within the context of McCoy's profession, the doctor proceeds with a characteristic attention to detail, which often functions at the expense of an understanding of underlying principles. In *Bread and Circuses* we see Spock commenting that he thought the doctor's remedies were often the result of luck. And, indeed, in *Elaan of Troyius* we see him proceeding by trial and error in his search for an antidote to Elaan's tears, with their love-potion effect. In *Spock's Brain,* McCoy is the one to replace the high priestess in the communicating device and receive "the old knowledge" from the "teacher." Under its impact, he suddenly sees a unifying principle which makes the replacement of Spock's brain look like child's play. During the operation the effect of the "teacher" wears off, and his characteristic approach brings him to a halt: he is bewildered by a profusion of detail. Kirk suggests he connect Spock's vocal chords and the first officer proceeds to direct the completion of the operation by which his own brain is restored to him.

McCoy and Women

In two episodes, *Shore Leave* and *This Side of Paradise,* we have the opportunity to view McCoy as well as others from projections of their fantasies which frequently involve women. In *Shore Leave* the thoughts of each individual materialize before his/her eyes. Kirk encounters a former rival and then Ruth, a former lover; McCoy sees first the white rabbit from *Alice in Wonderland* and ends the episode with two lavish Playboy bunnies on his arm. He was never one to favor sublimation. In *This Side of Paradise* an idyllic situation elicits the inner man: Spock is with Leila atempting to relate to the feminine within himself; Kirk is wrestling with his love and responsibility for the *Enterprise*; McCoy, the eternal bon-vivant, dreams of a mint julep. Lacking a certain intellectual seriousness, McCoy falls from time to time into the trivial and idiosyncratic, characteristics traditionally attributed to women.

McCoy frequently interacts with female characters on his trips into past worlds. Although appalled at the primitive surgical practices of the 1930s in *The City on the Edge of Forever,* he is sometimes impressed with the medical skill of women in relatively primitive cultures. In *A Private Little War,* Nona, the witch healer, can do with herbs what McCoy cannot; he wants to bring her secrets from the past back to the *Enterprise*. In *Friday's Child*, he functions as mid-wife and delivers a baby to a woman at first horrified at the intervention of a male, then impressed by his techniques. After delivering the baby, McCoy must teach her what to do with it. We can see emerging here the way in which the profession of physician took over and preempted the positive elements in the ancient healing arts which were once the preserve of women.

In medieval Switzerland a witch was called the "Bonne Femme" or "Bonne Dame," a precursor of the "sage-femme" who still functions in some places as a mid-wife. They were once the ones who knew the secrets of nature which could be used to cure as well as manipulate. Nona cures Kirk but would keep the captain under her control. Her services are not available for a fixed sum as are those of the professional physician. Further back in time than Medieval Europe, we glimpse priestesses presiding over arcane secrets and controlling the fate of their subjects.

As men developed and professionalized more effective healing techniques, making them accessible to all for a fair price, witches, mostly female, became the locus of residual negativity. In *A Private Little War*, Nona both cures and controls Kirk with her potions; in *Catspaw* the witch is an empty person craving sensation and knowledge for which she will manipulate anyone any way she can. Her command of nature is no longer curative of self or others but only self-seeking and illusory.

McCoy's Feminine Faculties

Although the feminine has been traditionally associated with women, McCoy emerges through many episodes as a repository of the positive feminine from the past. Similarly, his own personality depends largely on the feminine faculties of feeling and intuition. Although trained to measure, analyze and calculate, his instinctive responses are emotional and intuitive. His outbursts of "You can't do that" punctuate probably a third of the episodes. In addition to being an emotional person, McCoy values feeling, as we have seen in relation to his ideal of humanitarianism. He is true to his Judeo-Christian heritage in believing that, in and of itself, feeling is valuable since it includes the supreme good—love. Nonetheless, he is aware that emotion as such includes negative as well as positive feelings. He warns Flint in *Requiem for Methuselah* that Reena's new-found feelings will include the full range, not just "desirable" ones. McCoy himself acts out a comparable range of feeling when, despite his moral goodness and perhaps even because of it, he is eager to exterminate the blatantly evil Klingons in *Day of the Dove*.

Just as his humanistic concern for the whole person conflicts with our ideal of the physician as a scientific medical specialist, so his "feminine" emotional personality conflicts with his "masculine" professional training. Similarly, both his personality and values put him in frequent conflict with Spock, whom he criticizes as a mere computer. Not only do their temperaments differ but so do their values. *The Paradise Syndrome* presents us with the unusual situation of Spock and McCoy on the *Enterprise* without Kirk. Without the intermediary presence of the captain, McCoy reveals the variety of his feelings more clearly. His first reaction to Spock's decision to intercept the asteroid is open hostility. He accusingly complains that they cannot leave the captain on the planet since he might be needing them at that very moment. The impassioned tone of voice reveals the gulf which separates him from Spock, whose reasons for taking the calculated risk finally dominate. Later on, however, McCoy's criticisms focus on the strain Spock subjects himself to as he stays awake nights attempting to decipher the hieroglyphs. Although he "psychologizes" Spock's activity as an expression of the guilt he must feel for overstraining the engines of the *Enterprise,* he nonetheless finally makes contact with him through his role of the physician who must care for the crew.

In *The Tholian Web* we again see Spock in command and, as always, in conflict with McCoy. We hear the supposedly dead Kirk commending the *Enterprise* to Spock (by means of a prerecorded video tape) but at the same time reminding him that he should rely on McCoy for his human intuition. This particular capacity extends McCoy's commitment to the feminine faculties of feeling and intuition to include relying on the hunch as a means of knowing. In *Dagger of the Mind,* McCoy's intuition that Dr. Adams is not telling the truth about Van Gelder's derangement is what provokes Kirk's investigation, which in turn generates the central plot of the episode.

In *All Our Yesterdays*, McCoy and Spock are stranded in the ice-age cavern of Zarabeth who, like most of her fellow females, finds Spock very attractive. She had had no previous visitors and in her loneliness distorts the information she gives Spock about their situation. Spock identifies with her solitude and believes her statement that they cannot leave. He cannot suspect her of having lied but can only deal in his customarily logical way with the data as presented. McCoy, on the other hand, with his familiarity with human weakness, can suspect her motives and statements. Through questioning her, he unravels the truth necessary for them to escape. In this situation the usual relation of Spock to McCoy is reversed, since the doctor saves the science officer through his intuition. In a similar vein, Spock turns to McCoy in *Obsession* when confronted with a phenomenon his logic cannot handle: Kirk's apparent obsession to hunt and destroy a cosmic vampire.

McCoy's Ethnocentricity

McCoy's distrust of human nature is not unique to *All Our Yesterdays*; we also see it in *Return to Tomorrow*, in which he advises Kirk against letting Sargon borrow his body. His knowledge of the body includes awareness of its power to skew human judgments and infringe on the "good." As he says in *The Omega Glory*, the good must be awfully careful if it is to win. The skepticism we see in relation to humans is only increased in relation to aliens. Although he will defend Spock's unusual anatomy against external threat, as he does at the end of *The Omega Glory*, he is most frequently found complaining about it within the family of the *Enterprise*. If only Spock's blood were not green, he would not have an upset stomach from McCoy's medicine. If only his heart were in the right place and not where his liver ought to be. . . . When asked to minister to a creature as alien as a horta in *The Devil in the Dark*, McCoy is indignant. He is not a bricklayer! When he does minister to an alien life form which has temporarily assumed a human body in *By Any Other Name*, he adopts a smugly superior "we," as his patient is quick to point out.

Just as his values recall our cultural past, so they maintain our Western ethnocentricity. The biblical concept of love involves self-sacrifice and fellowship with people who have become "familiars" through conversion. The unconverted are dismissed as pagan or heathen. Under such a conception there is little room for aliens, including Vulcans, to lead their own lives on their own principles. Love as self-sacrifice is an idea which unifies those who hold it to be true while separating them from the "others."

McCoy, besides his loyalty to the ideal of love as self-sacrifice, also feels and tries to make others feel the guilt which is the inevitable result of the inevitable failure to live up to the ideal. In *The Corbomite Manoeuver*, when we see Kirk in an authoritarian light, McCoy is right there to remind him of ways in which he has neglected Bailey's personal situation. Whenever Spock must assume command, McCoy attacks him for having acted on ambition or attempts to undermine his confidence by inducing feelings of guilt. It is as if McCoy cannot tolerate too much assertion of self, even when it is necessary to the *Enterprise*. Love as self-sacrifice prefers the ease of unconscious union.

He is consistent in applying the same principles to himself: in *The Empath* he will not permit another to risk her life for him even to save himself. In a similar vein, he always apologizes to Spock after one of his emotional outbursts, for example, in *The Tholian Web*, *The Paradise Syndrome*, or *Bread and Circuses*, implying that internal guilt feelings function as part of his asserting even his "good" emotional tendencies. Once self-sacrifice has been accepted, perhaps guilt attached to self-assertion is its negative counterpart. Thus McCoy the physician is also McCoy the accuser, and McCoy as distillation of the past is also McCoy the spectre of past mistakes.

In looking back over the character of McCoy, we see a personality characterized by emotion and intuition, a professional commitment to caring for the physical and emotional health of others, a personal commitment to the inherited notions of self-sacrificing love and guilt. In Jungian terms, emotion and intuition characterize the feminine or unconscious mind and also are typical of the person oriented toward traditional religious values. In short, on several levels we have McCoy as "Mother."

Just as care of the body and feelings of others is traditionally the concern of Mother, so she is the conserver of the social order, the body politic. Mother conserves traditions, keeps the home fires glowing, and binds the wounds of the men who do the world's battles. Her world is defined by kitchen, children, and church. McCoy's church is implicit in his support of traditional Judeo-Christian values; his children are the crew of the *Enterprise*; his kitchen is the laboratory in which medicines to restore bodily well-being are synthesized. Even the ship's food is synthesized without the loving care McCoy gives to his remedies; thus he mediates between those feminine aspects of the starship as nurturing vessel and the crew being cared for.

Just as part of McCoy's femininity reflected an ethnocentric emphasis on Western tradition, so the very idea of Mother transmitted by him is culture-bound. We see McCoy in *Friday's Child* deliver the baby of a woman from another culture where the more primitive practices of midwives are the norm. Since children there are the property of men, the woman does not want her child; thus McCoy must not only deliver the baby but teach her mothering as well. He begins by trying to convince her that the child is hers, that men should not "take all the credit," and continues to show her how to hold it and talk to it. He is the mediator, not only between the physical mother and child, but between Motherhood and Childhood, between the mother and her traditional mothering role. Although Motherhood is often considered to be the essence of femininity in the West, it is clear in this episode that our usual idea of both the mother and the feminine is specific to our culture. This episode of *Star Trek* has taken us to another planet and in doing so has revealed to us that the notion of the feminine Mother is itself no more natural or universal than our ideas of nature. It is a culturally defined concept which need not apply to all women, just as our ideas of the natural need not apply to all planets. It is not inappropriate that McCoy, a man, embodies the Western ideal of the feminine Mother. It was after all an ideal made by men, not by women.

The Limitations of McCoy

The limitations of identifying the feminine with females becomes clear in *Turnabout Intruder*. Here, Dr. Janice Lester has exchanged bodies with Kirk. Although we as viewers know that Kirk's body has been possessed by her mind, nothing in McCoy's personality, training, or equipment can verify this. As he does not take mind seriously, neither can his instruments penetrate this most profound human attribute. Spock, on the other hand, through the Vulcan mind-meld can contact the consciousness of Kirk captive in the body of Janice Lester. McCoy so identifies a person with his or her body that he cannot grasp the inner person as distinct from, and perhaps opposed to, the outer shell. Janice Lester herself, vicious as she has become through multiple frustrations, may provide a useful perspective on women in our culture worthy of comment later on.

We need to reflect a bit on the feminine in McCoy and McCoy as feminine. Although his emotional personality and the nurturing functions which he performs evoke femininity, his medical training, conscious and masculine in tendency, justifies through his official job his presence on the *Enterprise*. Conflict seems inevitable, yet tension between opposing forces as well as their union, gives the *Enterprise* its impact. Just as matter/antimatter engines fire the starship, so the on-going tension between McCoy, the Mother, and McCoy, the Scientist, gives both three-dimensionality and vitality to the character. A comparable three-dimensionality emerges in the relations between Spock, Kirk, and McCoy, who make one family if not, at times, one personality. With Spock, however, we can jettison guilt as a specter of the past and a cumbersome human emotion in favor of acceptance and self-affirmation. With Spock we can move within our bodies and, through the mind-meld, beyond them to find a truer identity. Through the continuing tensions between Spock and McCoy energy is released which, through Spock, is set on a trajectory towards the future.

There is a place where no Truthsayer can see. We are repelled by it, terrorized. It is said a man will come some day. . . . He will look where we cannot—into both feminine and masculine pasts.

Frank Herbert

4 Spock: Catalyst for the Future

McCoy attends to the body; Spock deals with the mind. McCoy is emotional, Spock intellectual; McCoy is familiar, Spock alien. Nonetheless, McCoy is outside the command hierarchy, Spock is the first officer. Not only has an alien been accepted into the magic circle of the *Enterprise*, but he is second only to the captain. Although we need McCoy as we need our bodies, we need Spock to penetrate inner identities and to communicate with radically alien beings. We may appreciate McCoy for what he embodies of our past, but it is Spock who opens our way to the future.

Humans that we are, we cannot know pure mind. Thus we need Spock's physical and social heritage, as well as his interaction with McCoy and other characters to make him comprehensible to us. As we all know, Spock comes from Vulcan, the son of Sarek, a Vulcan astrophysicist and long-time diplomat. Spock's mother, however, is a human who chose to live on Vulcan as Sarek's wife; she is Amanda, whose name, from the Latin, means "worthy to be loved." In Spock's parents we find dramatized his inner conflict: Vulcan intellect versus human feeling.

Vulcan Physique

The word *Vulcan* itself typifies what has traditionally been associated with the masculine. Vulcan was the smith of the Roman gods—master of fire. Fire was associated with male deities even before Jehovah spoke from the burning bush. and in certain African tribes the smith is considered the first son of God because he can transmit the use of fire. Later, from classical antiquity to the Renaissance, fire was identified as a masculine element. Fire with its heat and light transforms matter and illuminates darkness. The planet Vulcan is characterized by a thin atmosphere which intensifies the heat and the light there. Vulcan physiology has adapted to these conditions and Vulcans can therefore cope with greater heat, light, and dryness than can humans. Due to the atmosphere on his home planet, Spock has pointed ears, which are better able to pick up attenuated sound waves. Hence, in *Operation Annihilate,* Spock's super-sensitive hearing is revealed when he overhears McCoy complimenting him to the captain. In the same episode, Spock's eyes are shown to have a second protective covering which filters excessive light. As we see through the reactions of Henoch in *Return to Tomorrow*, Spock's physical strength and his sensory organs are superior in every way to those of humans.

The enhanced masculinity of the Vulcan body is made explicit in the ritual of *pon farr*. Regardless of his sexual activity in the interim, every seven years an adult Vulcan male will be overwhelmed by the mating urge. At this time he loses all control of his fate and risks death unless restored by the traditional rituals surrounding *pon farr*. Interestingly enough, these rituals do not necessarily involve sexual or even physical contact between the partners. As we see in *Amok Time*, Spock is subjected to combat unto death with an opponent chosen by his reluctant fiancée. If she had not challenged their childhood betrothal, they would presumably have consummated their marriage, but she did not want to live the legend Spock had become, even among Vulcans. Hence she exercises the choices open to her to free herself. What we see in this episode contains no explicit sexuality, which on the one hand leaves all the more to the fervid imaginations of Spock's fans, and on the other hand suggests something important, perhaps, about the psychological significance of sexuality. Let's look in more detail at the episode.

Vulcan Sexuality: *Amok Time*

T'Pring, since she does not want to honor her childhood betrothal to Spock, chooses Kirk to be Spock's opponent because, whichever one of them wins, he will not marry her. Kirk would not want a Vulcan woman and Spock would not want her once she spurned him by demanding the challenge. She will be free to marry the man of her choice, whose life will not have been jeopardized in combat. Even Spock commends her logic. The ritual is presided over by T'Pau, the Vulcan matriarch so powerful that she alone among rulers declined a seat on the Federation Council. T'Pau and T'Pring together present a unified female presence which expresses itself through loyalty to traditional formulas. Under the eyes of female presence, Spock and Kirk do their battle.

Kirk is not only Spock's most treasured friend but also a father-figure. It was for Star Fleet, symbolized by Kirk as Captain of the *Enterprise*, that Spock left Vulcan and his father, Sarek, whose knowledge of computers is now, through Spock, at the service of Star Fleet rather than Vulcan. Sarek's reluctance to speak to his "prodigal son," as in *Journey to Babel,* is an expression—in human analogy at least—of the disapproval he must feel toward Spock for his new loyalty: Spock has, in effect, rejected Sarek for Star Fleet and Kirk.

Thus in *Amok Time* we witness a female presence combining a matriarch-mother and a fiancée-daughter, for and before whom Spock takes part in a ritual slaying of the father. Psychologically speaking, slaying the father means separating himself definitively from the male child's instinctive identification with him. It signifies a final coming into possession of himself as an independent person. We have here a psychologically potent metaphor for Spock's already established superiority of sensory and intellectual equipment, for his consummate masculinity. Completing this ritual releases Spock from the overwhelming mating urge just as effectively as the consummation of marriage would be expected to do.

Vulcan Mentality

Spock's mental superiority is related to his physical prowess. Only his mind, in fact, can control a body even as strong as his. When another and weaker mind inhabits it, we see the implication of such superiority. Henoch in *Return to Tomorrow* is such a lesser being who, once inside Spock's body, wants to keep it and use it to seduce or overpower others so that he can take over the *Enterprise*. Spock, on the other hand, is firmly the master of his body. He can control pain as we see in *Operation Annihilate*; he can by concentration aid his body's recuperative powers as we see in *A Private Little War*. Above all he can, under normal conditions, control his emotions. Even when momentarily overcome by some unknown biochemical force as in *The Naked Time* or *Plato's Stepchildren*, he recovers his control and in the latter even resists desire for revenge.

The most obvious example of Spock's superiority is his ability to compute complex mathematical problems rapidly, to read directly from the computer, to ingest written material with great speed and to have on instant recall an inner memory bank. We see these attributes in almost every episode. One of the most far-reaching of

Spock's mental abilities is the Vulcan mind-meld.[1] Through concentration, direct mental contact can be established with other beings. In *The Apple*, Spock knows when they are being watched; in *The Immunity Syndrome* he knows immediately and instinctively when the *Intrepid* and all of its Vulcan crew have been destroyed. In addition, by means of a touch, a veritable "laying-on-of-hands," Spock can communicate directly and complexly with a variety of creatures ranging from the horta, the living rock creature of *The Devil in the Dark,* to Nomad, the bossy computer in *The Changeling*.

Vulcan training provides a crucial link between Spock's superior sensory equipment and his mental powers. As he explains in *Is There in Truth No Beauty?* Vulcans have techniques to screen out distracting sensory data, including the movements of others' minds. By practicing such concentration, they can use their physical superiority without being dominated by it. Such concentration permits contact with the unknown and unconscious and also favors shared moments of true intimacy through the mingling of minds, like that between Spock and the Romulan captain in

1. This technique permits Vulcans to make direct and total mind-to-mind contact with another being. It was developed in *Dagger of the Mind* to resolve a dramatic situation in which Spock must make contact with the incoherent Dr. van Gelder. Hypnosis had been suggested in the script as the obvious technique, but the network refused to allow hypnosis to be practiced by characters who were not licensed physicians. Therefore, the Vulcan mind-meld, such an essential part of Spock's mental abilities, was developed in response to a conflict with the network.

The Enterprise Incident. Concentration is, after all, both a screening out and a tuning in. Spock's mental powers are under such control that they can flow out, unseen, in the desired channels and connect the inner Spock with life throughout the universe.

Spock in Command: *The Galileo Seven*

As second in command, Spock has occasions when he must take over the *Enterprise.* McCoy lacks the self-assertion to command, as well as the intellectual foresight necessary for long-range strategic planning. Spock has greater capacities, which we see tested in *The Galileo Seven.* The episode opens with Spock commanding the shuttlecraft *Galileo* on a research mission. The craft is pulled off course to a planet where Spock and his crew must cope with giant and savage humanoids who hamper their attempts to repair the *Galileo.*

He approaches the mission with impeccable logic, which irritates several crewmen to insolence and costs the lives of more than one. Although the crew members of the *Galileo* have demonstrated to the natives their superior weaponry, the latter—illogically—continue to attack. When a crewman is killed, the human survivors insist on burying him despite the risks. Spock agrees with reluctance, only to be saved himself by crew members acting out of the same human, illogical, fellow-feeling. After the shuttlecraft takes off, they appear to be doomed to burn up in the planet's atmosphere when Spock jettisons the remaining fuel and ignites it as an emergency flare. McCoy, true to form, accuses Spock of imposing foolhardy suicide on all of them. This last act of desperation, however, attracts the *Enterprise,* which beams them aboard just as the shuttlecraft disintegrates. Spock has met the challenge of an irrational universe despite the discontent of his crew. In explaining his daring act, Spock asserts that in a desperate situation for which logic can find no solution, an act of desperation is the only logical response. If the heart can have its reasons, reason can have its own kind of heart.

Spock Versus McCoy

Spock's visibility as a character is especially obvious in relation to McCoy, his chief critic and antagonist. McCoy, as we have seen, is the advocate of emotion to whom Spock is often a kind of subhuman computer. The doctor is frequently annoyed when Spock calculates the odds; he mistrusts Spock's use of logic in solving problems; he finds the peculiarities of Vulcan physiology an unnecessary inconvenience, especially when he himself appears less knowledgeable about them than Spock or Sarek themselves. However, his attacks on Spock for lack of feeling are sometimes countered by Spock in such a way as to indicate that his emotions, like his heart, are not missing but only located in different places. Reason can have its feelings, though they may not coincide with those foreseen in our Western cultural stereotypes.

As we have seen in this chapter on McCoy, the doctor is emotional and intuitive in his immediate reactions. He is concerned with human feelings and their implications and thus represents the unconscious mind, which functions spontaneously and unselfconsciously. His Judeo-Christian humanitarian values downgrade self-awareness and self-assertion in favor of self-sacrifice and love as unselfconscious union. McCoy's ideal heterosexual love is best expressed in *For the Earth is Hollow and I Have Touched the Sky*. Here, stricken with a fatal disease, McCoy falls in love with a priestess intent on her duty of implementing the wishes of the ancestors which are embodied in a computer. He wants to remain with her and devote his services to her people. In order to marry her he accepts the Instrument of Obedience, which permits no dissent from the accepted program. Love as self-sacrifice is thus expressed as devotion to duty as a physician and as loyalty to a past, permitting unconscious union with fellow followers. To Spock is left the job of deciphering and repairing the computer's program so that he can save both the spaceship and McCoy from destruction. McCoy is at home in the world of our cultural past, ethnocentrically disseminating earthly conceptions around the galaxy.

Mind Versus Emotion

Spock, on the other hand, is supremely conscious. In Jungian terms, he is a sensation and thinking type, a model representative of the attributes of the masculine or conscious mind. As we have seen, the superiority of his sensory and intellectual equipment helps him to value logic and mental control as the means of civilizing the savagery of emotion. As he says in *The Apple,* more murders have been committed on earth in the name of love than for any other motive. Love and other spontaneous emotions are by no means unmitigatedly good; love is part of the vast range of feelings which must include its opposite— hate. If we choose to seek out and value love, we must be as careful as if it were the tip of an unseen iceberg. And as we saw in *Amok Time,* even heterosexual love has for Spock been sublimated into symbolic ritual actions which relieve his mind and ultimately his body by freeing him from *pon farr.* He is thereby released from tensions that would, if they remained on a purely physical level, be relieved only by sexual intercourse.

Spock and Human Love

In Spock, sexual contact has been transformed into a metaphor based on psychic significance rather than on physical activity. Similarly, traditional heterosexual love becomes through Spock more spiritual than physical. On board the *Enterprise,* we see his attractiveness to Nurse Chapel in several episodes. In *A Private Little War,* she savors the closeness permitted through tending his wounds; in *Amok Time,* she welcomes the opportunity to care for him, to prepare his favorite soup. Whereas these episodes use traditional postures for heterosexual caring which assimilate the woman to a mother-figure,

Return to Tomorrow offers a new vision of union.

In this episode, Henoch, Sargon, and Thalassa, who lack bodies, have borrowed those of Spock, Kirk, and Dr. Ann Mulhall for long enough to build themselves android bodies. Henoch, sensing immediately the superiority of Spock's body, lays his plans to break the agreement to return the body to Spock. The ball in which Spock's mind is temporarily stored is broken and we fear that Spock, the real Spock, has died. Nurse Chapel, however, has harbored his mind in her body, which gives her the mental control necessary to resist Henoch's suggestions and to decide to give the fatal shot to him, thereby chasing him from Spock's body. If one meaning of intercourse is the sharing of bodies as a means of sharing minds, we have here an image for a more profound sharing than can be had through a mingling of bodily fluids. Those secret places lovers long to reach through the body can be reached more directly through the mind. As in the rituals of *pon farr*, Spock helps transmute love from physical to psychic significance.

In other episodes, we see Spock in relation to women outside of the *Enterprise*. In *All Our Yesterdays*, Zarabeth wants to keep Spock with her and distorts the truth in her attempt to do so. Spock seems to identify with her solitude and in retrospect feels she drew him to a more primitive stratum of the Vulcan psyche. As Zarabeth appeals to the instincts of Spock, Leila in *This Side of Paradise* appeals to the emotions. As she reveals to the colony's leader, Sandoval, she has met Spock before and wants him. She exposes Spock to the spores which she as the colony's botanist has discovered. Under their influence we see Spock with his head in Leila's lap enjoying his feelings and intuitions as they find shapes in the passing clouds. As McCoy and the *Enterprise* save Spock from Zarabeth, so Kirk and the *Enterprise* free him from the spores.

As in these two episodes the women wanted in some way to "have" Spock, so in *Spock's Brain* we see Kara, a high priestess, steal his most important organ. She represents an underground world of females who have not integrated the mind into their beings and thus must steal a superior brain from outside. She, who lives farthest from the airborne world where Spock is at home, is desperate to steal the most crucial part of his body. Once again Spock is rescued by Kirk and McCoy.

Spock and Romulan Love: *The Enterprise Incident*

This episode develops Spock's most significant contact with the opposite sex in the exciting context of a spying mission. In fact, this is the only time a relationship develops between Spock and a woman independently of magic spores, time machines, *pon farr*, viruses, or other extrinsic influences. The Romulans and the Federation are approximate equals in power who, as a result, are strongly jealous of any slight gain on one side or the other. Hence Star Fleet orders the *Enterprise* to steal from the Romulans their new cloaking device which might allow them to intrude unnoticed into Federation space.

The *Enterprise* penetrates Romulan territory and is predictably surrounded. Kirk and Spock beam aboard the Romulan vessel, where Spock, apparently attracted by the beautiful female commander and her offer of partnership and eventually a Romulan command position, appears to kill Kirk by means of the Vulcan death grip. McCoy takes the body of Kirk back to the *Enterprise* where the captain is revived and disguised as a Romulan. The rest of the drama is played out on the Romulan ship where Kirk is finally successful in stealing the cloaking device while Spock's interchanges with the Romulan commander keep her occupied. As Spock, whose ploy has been discovered, is making his final, long-winded death statement, he along with the Romulan commander is beamed aboard the *Enterprise* for a triumphant escape.

On board, Spock and the woman have one final scene together. As the two have shared ancestors common to Vulcans and Romulans and have exchanged names unintended for human ears, so they have participated in direct mental communion which is their secret and will be, Spock hopes, more lasting than the secrets of the military technology to which their bodies and duties are dedicated. As mutual attraction served as a cloak for spying, so spying became a cloaking device for personal encounter. Kirk has his secret, the Romulan cloaking device; the Romulan captain has hers, inner contact with Spock. Neither she nor Spock needs more than a glance or a hand to accomplish the union of their minds; their fingers perform the ballet humans need the whole body for.

Spock and Fellow-Feeling

To McCoy, these significant exchanges between Spock and Nurse Chapel and between him and the Romulan commander would not qualify as emotional in the traditional sense. Although McCoy most often draws our attention to where Spock's feelings are *not*, on rare occasions he helps us to locate where they are.

In *Bread and Circuses,* when McCoy and Spock are in jail, McCoy's attack on Spock's presumed lack of feeling makes the latter's worried nagging at the bars all the more eloquent. Even McCoy finally recognizes that Spock in his own way is expressing anxiety about Kirk. In *Spectre of the Gun,* when McCoy and Spock along with Kirk and Scott are recovering from the shock of Chekov's shooting, McCoy accuses Spock of thinking about technical problems instead of mourning for the presumably dead Chekov. Spock reminds them that he is half-human and also figures out the significance for them of Chekov's apparent death. Although they have been thrust into the past as the Clanton gang of Tombstone, Arizona, which was shot to death, Spock shows them they have a chance for survival since the Clanton "played" by Chekov did not die that day. What they take to be the imperative of history is not binding on them. Spock's dedicated clarity of mind is all the more impressive since an earlier episode, *Tomorrow is Yesterday*, recreated a situation which led everyone to believe that history had to repeat itself.

Whereas McCoy's love was unconscious union, Spock's is based on conscious differentiation; whereas McCoy's link to the *Enterprise* is through his profession, Spock's is through loyalty. As we all realize, Spock with his superior powers could simply dominate humans: seduce the women, overpower the men. With his training, he could more easily, and with the blessing of his father, be working on Vulcan. He has chosen to work for the Federation and to open new worlds to men by making his capacities available to them. In *Journey to Babel* he confronts his mother who rejects the logic of placing loyalty to the *Enterprise* above his biological family; in his hybrid aloneness he also shares with her the kind of solitude she feels among Vulcans. Through his choice of career and his loyalty to it, he is relating on a larger scale to that which his mother represents: emotions, intuitions, the unconscious mind, the unknown. Just as he reenacted in *Amok Time* a conscious symbol for the significance of mating, so he repeats symbolically in *Journey to Babel* a Vulcan commitment to humans such as the one that must have joined Sarek to Amanda. Though conscious and logical, such a commitment is nonetheless—and perhaps all the more—love.

There are other still more eloquent expressions of Spock's compassionate love. In *Requiem for Methuselah*, the final scene sees Kirk mourning the death of Reena for which he feels responsible. Spock with a nerve pinch[2] lets him get some needed sleep. McCoy delivers his habitual sermon to Spock on the latter's inability to comprehend Kirk's feelings, then leaves saying how he wishes Kirk could forget. Spock—with a mind-meld—gives the captain saving forgetfulness. Similarly, it is Spock in *Obsession* who spontaneously goes to the cabin of Ensign Garrovick and, by reassuring him that fear before the unknown is entirely normal, helps to free him from paralyzing guilt. How much more effective this is than McCoy's command that the ensign EAT. Spock's attention and understanding seem far more loving than McCoy's accusations and more constructive than letting the Ensign wallow in feelings of guilt.

Spock and Compassion: *The Menagerie*

The lengths to which Spock will go for love of another is best portrayed in *The Menagerie*. Here Spock receives direct mental communication from the Talosians, who inform him that his former captain, Pike, has been seriously disabled in an accident. Having used his superior mental powers to grasp another's situation and needs, Spock asserts his independence by adjusting the ship's computers, as only he can do, in order to divert the *Enterprise* to the Starbase where Pike is. The mutiny continues as he arranges to have

2. By means of the Vulcan nerve pinch, Spock can easily render anyone unconscious by pinching the neck or shoulder. Leonard Nimoy invented the technique as a means of coping dramatically with the negative Kirk in *The Enemy Within*.

Pike taken aboard and the starship set on an unalterable course for Talus IV, the one planet forever forbidden to the Federation on pain of death. Many years before, Spock had accompanied Pike to this planet, where the power of illusion is strong enough to create whatever is desired. In returning there Spock will be permitting Pike to join Vina, a woman who though physically disfigured by the crash which put her there, can seem beautiful, thanks to illusion. Pike, once he arrives, will similarly be transformed into the handsome young man Vina fell in love with. Together they will share the rest of their days in the happy illusion of health and wholeness. Spock's mutiny was a calculated risk, putting self-assertion and consciousness at the service of love, but a love better characterized as active, careful attention than what is commonly called emotion.

In most episodes Spock provides the key to resolving the situation: he intervenes with the information and understanding necessary for the captain to make his decision. Through his superior mental powers the *Enterprise* can reach out to and cope with the unknown. In *The Menagerie*, however, Spock takes over the starship and guides it on the basis of what only he can know. The drama unfolds in the conflict between his world and that which is generally available to humans. A planet such as Talus IV is forbidden to men since the power of mind so dominates there that they lose their grasp on "reality." The death penalty hangs over those who dare go there, as if to say that they will be forever lost to humankind. By acting on the mental powers that set him apart, Spock again risks death and disgrace through mutiny. He ventures where no man *should* go and *returns.*

Spock as Mediator

As we have seen in relation to *The Menagerie,* what is beyond human capacities, what is unconscious or unknown, is forbidden and often considered evil. Madness, the result of losing one's grip on reality, of losing oneself in illusion, was traditionally considered possession by the devil. The universe is quickly moralized and that which *is* unknown becomes that which *ought to be* unknown. Spock as half-human and half-Vulcan can both reach out to the unknown and relate it to what we know. He is central to the *Enterprise,* if not its center, because, confronted by a world polarized into the known and unknown, we are also confronted by a paradox: the conscious mind can only know the unknown in so far as it is known. Like the archetype Number, Spock can have access to both worlds, the transcendent and the immanent, the unknown and the known. As a hybrid, his structure reflects a kind of equation: one half plus one half. Through his Vulcan mental powers he can directly contact aliens; through his human side he can make known what would otherwise remain in the dark.

Spock's superior mental powers are not only placed at the service of the Federation by means of aliens, as in *The Menagerie,* but also made available to aliens by means of the *Enterprise's* mission. As Spock saved Pike from the darkness of paralysis, so he saved the horta from extinction. In *The Devil in the Dark,* the *Enterprise* is called to the rescue of a mining colony afflicted with a man-eating demon in its underground tunnels. It dissolves men, machinery, and rock as if it were a smouldering fragment of hell. Spock, however, by means of the mind-meld establishes contact with it, wounded though it has been by Kirk. He learns that she is a long-time resident of the planet who had happily coexisted with the miners until they broke into the chamber where her species' eggs are kept. She is in fact the last horta and caretaker of the eggs which will hatch into the new generation. Like Spock she is a mediator. If the miners will leave her eggs alone, she, along with the children will continue to live peaceably underground, eating the rock that is their food and thereby making tunnels for the miners. As an agreement is reached between the miners and the horta, a new bridge is built between the known and the unknown.

As Spock performs the mind-meld with the horta, he makes visible her pain, which is partly due to her wound, but also partly due to her isolation. She is alone among aliens, at least until her eggs hatch. Similarly Spock's mother, Amanda, is an emotional being alone among highly disciplined Vulcans, and Spock himself is a Vulcan alone among humans. Although the mind-meld results from the combination of Vulcan intellect and Vulcan training, its impact can have emotional resonance, as it relieves the pain of solitude. Unrelieved solitude is not only terrible to experience but can even be fatal, as we see in *Dagger of the Mind,* when Dr. Adams has his mind wiped clean by his machine at a time when there is no one in the control room to communicate new thoughts. Solitude, however, is but the other side of IDIC—infinite diversity in infinite combinations. With expanded consciousness and communication comes a new respect for the unfamiliar. Communion is not restricted to the converted but can now be extended to everyone in all their diversity. Although initially an intellectual phenomenon, Spock's mind-melding catalyzes new emotions and new ways of reacting as well as acting. Although half-human, perhaps because half-human, Spock is consummately humane. Supremely conscious, Spock is a link with the unconscious; archetypally masculine, he opens a new door for the feminine.

Because of Spock's special relationship with the feminine and the future, he has special importance for women. The unconscious as feminine has been idealized as the paradisal garden, the all-embracing Mother Nature. Similarly, its other face has been moralized into the evil temptress. Western images of women have suffered a parallel fate. From the mother whose all nourishing and impossible hospitality men dream of, emerges Eve, the prototypical female who becomes the temptress responsible for the fall of Adam and thus the human race. Given the sexual connotations of the serpent in the Eden myth, Eve in responding to it is asserting her individual sexuality. Just as Spock in *pon farr* had to fight the father-figure to overcome a child's identification with him, so for women, too, sexual assertion is a first step in psychological differentiation from the mother, the maternal paradise. Sexual awareness becomes a necessary step in the process of individuation.

Spock demythologizes Eden as we saw in *The Way to Eden* because he is willing to relate it sympathetically to consciousness rather than unconsciousness; similarly he demythologizes evil when he reveals to us the specter of the omnivorous mother, the devil-in-the-dark, as intelligent and sympathetic. In reaching out to the feminine, Spock neutralizes the myths and stereotypes that have helped keep it underground as diabolical or on a pedestal as heavenly. Similarly, Spock reaches very earthly and sometimes earthy female fans through his readily acknowledged sex appeal. As ideals of the feminine subside to ideas and assume more rich nuances, so women emerge into three-dimensional individuality capable of intellect, desire, and orientation toward the future.

Whenever a mind is simple
and receives a divine wisdom,
old things pass away—
means, teachers, texts, tem-
ples fall: it lives now and ab-
sorbs past and future with the
present hour.

Emerson

5 Kirk: Solution for the Present

Kirk is the agent for unifying opposing realities within the *Enterprise* and for transforming this tension into the energy needed to accomplish the ship's mission. Matter and antimatter, the familiar and the alien, are united within both ship and captain. Out of such unions come energy and direction. The mission of the starship is to explore new worlds and to go where no man has gone before—in other words to relate the known and the unknown on a large scale. The *Enterprise*, which functions on the energy generated through opposition within, becomes one term in a new opposition in space: the microcosm of human consciousness as it encounters the unknown or unconscious without or within.

We have seen the circle as symbolic of

wholeness, but the circle as *mandala* must have one additional attribute—a center. Around this center one can move in any direction. Without this focal point to provide structure, a circle would seem no more significant than the round opening of a garbage can. Oppositions can pile up, distort one another, cancel one another out. If the whole is greater than the sum of the parts, the increment comes from the structure which relates them to one another.

The structures most prominent in and on the *Enterprise* center on the relationships between opposing forces. In the shape of the starship itself we see the circular form complemented by the cigar-shaped sections of engineering and the propulsion units, in short a visual and spatial embodiment of the opposition of circular and linear, the potential for both containment and movement. Under Kirk's direction the *Enterprise* serves as a vehicle which can both contain the crew and move them through space in a purposeful manner. The starship is transformed from a visual image of opposition into a vehicle for resolution.

Kirk and the Resolution of Tension: And the Children Shall Lead

A comparable interplay of opposites occurs in diverse contexts on board. In the engineering section we have the matter/antimatter reactors which provide power to the ship. On the bridge we have the perpetual opposition between McCoy and Spock: McCoy, the Terran and distillation of our past; Spock, the half-alien and catalyst for the future. Feminine faculties confront their masculine counterparts. Just as Kirk transforms into directed activity the opposing principles implicit in the *Enterprise* as ship, so he unifies and directs the energy from engineering as well as the tensions between McCoy and Spock.

In *And the Children Shall Lead*, Kirk, Spock, and McCoy beam down to a Federation science colony. All the adults have committed suicide, yet the children seem very happy, as if nothing had happened. Kirk puts the orphaned children in the care of McCoy, whose first concern is with their emotional situation: although they have watched their parents die, they show no trace of grief. He fears the shock has produced a kind of amnesia which can be cured only by releasing the suppressed feelings. Health is for him physical and emotional wholeness and balance. Spock, on the other hand, hypothesizes an outside force which produced suicidal depression in the adults and which is continuing to influence the children through promise of reward. Some immaterial being must want them to behave as they do. Spock is concerned with the logical analysis of causes.

Spock picks up unknown life readings emanating from a cave which he and Kirk then explore and where Kirk has an attack of anxiety. Kirk feels Spock's life readings as emotional, but Spock's sensor cannot register Kirk's feelings; nonetheless they are both aware of an unseen presence, of a force apart from body. By way of contrast, McCoy's awareness of emotions is filtered through psychiatric textbooks. While Kirk and Spock explore, McCoy applies existing knowledge.

The children nearly succeed in taking over the *Enterprise* by awakening each crewman's "inner beast," his hidden fears. Only two officers are spared: Spock and McCoy. McCoy, being outside the chain of command, is permitted to go about his business. Spock at first does not perceive what is taking place since human emotions are on the periphery of this world. Nonetheless, when Kirk's speech becomes garbled and ineffective, Spock is snapped into awareness at the very moment Kirk is seized by his fear of losing command. Sustained by his Vulcan friend, Kirk regains control of himself by withstanding his "beast" in the light of consciousness bolstered by Spock's strength.

Freed on the personal level from the threat of the children, Kirk regains the bridge and resolves the episode by drawing on the perspectives provided by both Spock and McCoy. There *is* an evil force using the children through promise of reward, and there *are* blocked emotions within them. Kirk calls forth the evil spirit so that he can be perceived in the light of day; his evil, now trapped within himself, makes him ugly. Kirk also shows the children videotapes of their last days with their parents and in doing so releases the emotions which they had repressed.

Thus, we have a kind of model or paradigm for relationships found in many other episodes. Both Spock and McCoy contribute to what Kirk needs to resolve a situation. What Spock provides almost always relates in some way to his Vulcanness. Within the *mandala* of wholeness there must be room for the unknown, the unconscious, the alien. Spock, while central to the *Enterprise,* nonetheless leaves Kirk at its center.

Kirk and Wholeness: *The Lights of Zetar*

Kirk at the center of the bridge-*mandala* transforms opposition to energy and directs the *Enterprise's* course: he commands the coordinates of the ship's trajectory, he coordinates the skills and capacities of the crew. As he unifies others, so he as a character embodies an inner unity of personality. In Jung's terms, Kirk has access to all four psychological faculties.

Kirk as a whole person has access within himself to emotion and intuition, intellect and sensation. He can encounter the world either through sensation by registering the data which can convey concrete reality or through intuition by grasping the possibilities hidden in the background of the concrete. He can process or digest the fruit of this encounter by means of the intellect or rational analysis, or through emotional evaluation, which tells him how or to what extent something is important. The fullness of his access to these functions is symbolized by the presence, on one side, of Spock, committed to sensation and intellect, and on the other, McCoy, attuned to intuition and feeling.

As we have seen with Spock, sensation and intellect are considered attributes of the conscious or masculine mind; as we saw with McCoy, emotion and intuition are identified with the unconscious or feminine mind. Whereas each one had a dominant way of interacting with the world,

Kirk has access to both of their characteristic methods of approach. Whereas Spock is the archetypically masculine, Kirk is the perfectly well-rounded human male. If McCoy's feminine side makes him at times fussy and whimsical, Kirk's use of emotion and intuition is combined with a vigorous and accurate intellect.

Kirk's relation to the balanced diversity of the four faculties emerges most clearly in *The Lights of Zetar,* where each of them appears embodied in a single crew member. Where Kirk was unifier of the Spock-McCoy opposition in the preceding episode, here he is the bemused ego around whom McCoy and Spock, joined by Scott and Mira Romaine, center and harmonize. Through identifying each faculty as it is embodied in a separate character, we gain a clear perspective on the ways in which they complement one another.

The Lights of Zetar opens as a mysterious storm affects a different nerve center in each of the bridge crew: Kirk cannot speak, Uhura cannot hear, Sulu cannot move his arm. Mira Romaine, a Lieutenant on her first deep-space voyage, is rendered unconscious, and obscure growling sounds emerge from her throat independently of her consciousness. Kirk orders a complete medical examination of her in the hope of discovering why she alone is so affected. The storm goes on to destroy all life on Memory Alpha, a space research station built without defenses since its research library is freely open to all. We see the storm enter the ship's viewing screen from the left or west, continue through Memory Alpha, and exit to the right or east.

Inspecting damage on the library station, Kirk, McCoy, Spock, and Scott are joined by Mira Romaine, who has an overwhelming intuition that the storm is returning. Then Sulu confirms her hunch, and the crew returns to the safety of the ship. The west is the locus of sensation in Jung's conception and the storm first makes its presence known through the ship's sensors. The storm returns from the east, Jung's locus of intuition; only Mira's intuitive insight could perceive the renewed threat before it comes into sensor range.

The opposition of intuition and sensation as modes of receiving knowledge of the external world is represented in the characters of Mira and Scott. From the beginning of the episode they have been mutually attracted, as opposites often are; and their different reactions to the same events put their different modes of perception into relief. Mira as the intuitive one has premonitions of what will happen: she sees the dead men that are later found on Memory Alpha; she warns of the returning storm. These intuitions come to her as emanations from the unconscious which she cannot control. Scott, the devotee of the practical and the verifiable, a perfect Jungian sensation type, tries to explain away Mira's premonitions as space sickness, as an indication that she is not yet accustomed to deep space.

The complementary sets of opposites, representing different ways of digesting perceptions of the outside world, emerges in Spock and McCoy. Spock continues to analyze the data he receives from the sensors and ascertains that the storm is in fact a composite of ten distinct life forms whose acts are willful. McCoy, ever ready for emotional explanations, delves into the psychosomatic history of Mira Romaine and finds that she is unusually pliant in learning situations. Something in her emotional make-up must be contributing to her problem. Both Spock and McCoy, of course, have a piece of the truth.

As the episode evolves, we see how each of these crew members and each faculty contributes to the final resolution. Mira's newness to space is primary to Scott, who is devoted to "down-to-earth" explanations perceived through the Jungian faculty of sensation. She *is* susceptible to suggestion, a factor clear to McCoy's sensitivity to emotion. Spock by analyzing the situation reveals the identity of the Zetars as intelligent though bodiless beings and hypothesizes their inability to cope with gravitational pressure. Mira continues to receive intuitions culminating in a vision of Scott dying. Her resistance to this premonition foreshadows the conclusion, in which we see Scott risking touching her, despite his knowledge that the Zetars, who are in possession of her body, are dangerous. Scott counts on her expressed unwillingness to see him die as the saving factor as he puts her into a pressure chamber which can force the Zetars out of her. The increased gravitational pressure symbolically reinforces her own will to achieve the density of three-dimensional individual existence.

The final scene unites Spock, McCoy, Scott, and Mira: intellect, emotion, sensation, and intuition, as they inform the decision Kirk must make concerning whether or not Mira should be sent for therapy to a Star Base. Mira has spontane-

ously returned to her post as if intuiting the outcome of their decision; Scott informs the captain
that everything he can observe is just fine; McCoy
can think of no more positive influence on her
than Scott's love; Spock affirms that the act of
struggle will itself have served to strengthen her
ego. Kirk adds the comment that work is good
therapy and finds himself pleasantly surprised at
the luxury of simply ordaining what his subordi-
nates for once all agree upon. Mira can continue
as a functioning member of Star Fleet; she and
the *Enterprise* are simultaneously restored to
balance.

In the following episodes, Kirk solves problems by relying on his strength in one particular
faculty at a time. In the process, all the dimensions of his personality can be more fully appreciated.

Kirk and Intellect: *The Changeling*

A robot called Nomad attacks the *Enterprise*
and foils counterattack by absorbing the energy
of the photon torpedoes. On the *Enterprise* it
identifies Kirk as its creator and sets about helping him by eradicating imperfections and errors.
"Units" Scott and Uhura are put out of order for
displaying the imperfection of emotion; the entire
starship is almost destroyed when Nomad insists
that it function at maximum efficiency, hence at
speeds the ship was not made to withstand.

By means of a mind-meld, Spock establishes
that Nomad was created by a man whose name
resembles Kirk's. Nomad began as an earth probe
sent out to search for life forms; it long ago

collided with an alien probe whose mission was to sterilize soil samples. Nomad feels this encounter with the Other to have perfected him; hence he aggressively imposes "perfection" wherever he goes. Nomad's memory banks, although damaged, have assimilated into their content that of the Other.

Kirk acts on Spock's new information by assuming Nomad's two basic premises: that Nomad is perfect and that Kirk is its creator. Accepting his own humanity and hence imperfection, Kirk, through the logical exposition of these two premises, brings Nomad to a state of confusion and hence paralysis. While sorting through his memory banks for some clue to the resolution of this logical bind, Nomad is placed in the transporter and sent into outer space. Kirk has used his intellect with such expertise that he wins the commendation of Spock and the freedom to continue with the *Enterprise's* mission.

Kirk demonstrates similar intellectual prowess in coping with machine logic in such episodes as *The Ultimate Computer, The Return of the Archons,* and *What Are Little Girls Made Of?* He can even go so far as to consciously adopt illogic to burn out the androids of *I, Mudd*—a strategy which, needless to say, presumes high intelligence.

Kirk and Sensation: *The Conscience of the King*

Kirk and several others suspect that Karidian, a travelling actor, is really Kodos, who twenty years earlier killed much of the population

of Tarsus IV. A dwindling food supply convinced
Kodos that he must kill many people so that some
could survive. His decision was proved wrong by
the early arrival of a food shipment, and his
reputation for evil survives. Thomas Leighton,
Lieutenant Riley, and Kirk are the only surviving
witnesses of the massacre, and Leighton is killed
shortly after mentioning his suspicions to Kirk.
Kirk's computer check on Kodos-Karidian reveals
that the former's life disappears when the latter's
begins. After an attempt on Riley's life, Spock
discovers that all of the witnesses to the massacre
on Tarsus IV have died violently while the
Karidian acting troupe was nearby.

All the evidence points to the identity of
Kodos and Karidian, who now becomes a suspect
for the murders of the various witnesses. No one
would have criticized Kirk for seizing Karidian,
but Kirk insists on verifiable proof that Karidian
is indeed Kodos and that he murdered those who
might recognize him.

The dramatic situation resolves itself
through its own inner dynamics. Kodos is in fact
Karidian, but his daughter, whom he has at-
tempted to shield from the infamy of his past life,
has killed the witnesses and threatens Kirk's life.
Her father, horrified, steps into the phaser bolt
aimed at Kirk. Thus the father dies and Lenore,
the daughter, goes mad.

Kirk, by insisting on verifiable certainty
where human lives are at stake, has relied on the
faculty Jung calls sensation, which perceives and
collates tangible, proven evidence. Kirk's awareness of the power and importance of sensation is
especially crucial in *By Any Other Name,* where

the captain convinces the Kelvans to return the ship to him and his galaxy by stimulating the new and intriguing sensations possible in their unfamiliar human bodies. This same faculty is responsible for the practical inventiveness which allows Kirk to assemble a crude but effective mortar in *Arena*.

Kirk and Emotion: *This Side of Paradise*

The *Enterprise* has been ordered to rescue colonists on Omicron Ceti III, who have been exposed to deadly rays. On beaming down, they discover the colonists not only perfectly healthy but extraordiarily happy and content. Leila, the botanist, who has known and longed for Spock in the past, exposes him to plant spores which create a state of bliss. One by one all the crew is infected: McCoy dreams of mint juleps, Sulu digs half-heartedly in the garden, Spock lolls in the lap of Leila. Kirk alone resists their effect and finds himself alone on the *Enterprise*. No one will respect his commands or return to the starship. Finally he too is infected by some plants which were beamed aboard. He is about to beam down, leaving the *Enterprise* an empty hull in space when, while gathering his belongings, he comes across a medal, its pendant in the shape of a woman, reminding him of his love for the *Enterprise*. The strength of his feeling of devotion breaks the hold the spores have over him. Having freed himself, he calls Spock on board and taunts him until anger finally breaks the spores' hold on Spock. Together they beam subsonic sound waves at the planet in order to irritate the crew and the colonists till they snap out of their reveries. The colonists realize the insignificance of their accomplishments, though McCoy ascertains that thanks to the spores all have enjoyed superior health with no ill effect from the rays. The colonists will seek another planet where they will be uninfluenced by either rays or euphoric spores, and the *Enterprise* can continue on its mission.

While Kirk frequently resolves problems with computers on the strength of his intellect, here the solution arises spontaneously through the intensity of his feelings. In *This Side of Paradise* the saving emotions simply come to him. He cannot control them any more than McCoy can control his outbursts. *Court-Martial* is still another instance of his deeply felt attachment to the *Enterprise*. His character is remarkable for including both of the opposing faculties of conscious intellect and unconscious emotion.

Kirk and Intuition: *Obsession*

During an information-gathering visit to Argus X, Kirk's landing party is attacked by a gaseous cloud which leaves behind a sweet honey-like smell. Kirk is quick to perceive the smell with his senses but relies on intuitions from his unconscious mind to direct his response. He risks the appearance of madness as he follows the creature and his hunches across the galaxy.

At the first hint of the sweet odor, Spock offers the explanation that it is growing season on Argus X. Kirk, however, answers with associations from his past. Kirk recalls that he himself, eleven years earlier, faced this same situation.

At that time, he was serving with Captain Garrovick when a cloud emanating the same odor killed the captain and half of the crew. Kirk himself hesitated a moment before firing his phaser[1] and had never been sure if that moment's lapse had cost the lives of so many Federation crewmen. When the creature appears in this episode, young Ensign Garrovick similarly hesitates before firing and one man dies. Kirk blames the Ensign as he had blamed himself and confines him to quarters.

Spock plays a crucial role in fending off the creature and also controlling the inner monster, guilt. In Garrovick's cabin, Spock can safely shut out the creature because his blood contains copper-based hemocyan rather than the iron-based hemoglobin the creature feeds on. Similarly Spock can make the definitive move against both Kirk's and Garrovick's guilt by proving that phaser fire could have had no effect on the cloud. Thus neither of them need blame himself for a normal human hesitation.

On the one hand, this creature is a curse which consumes blood and destroys the physical man; on the other, it can destroy the inner man by consuming him in the curse of guilt and doubt. Potential conflict arises when unconscious forces cannot be publicly verified except by one with superior mental powers. Spock, of course, is such a person. He is able to perceive the creature in its external reality as a potential threat to the universe, and as a threat to the internal

1. This type of gun fires an energy beam whose force can be adjusted to stun or to kill. A Florida police force has apparently modeled a new weapon on the phaser.

equilibrium of the captain through its arousing of feelings of guilt. Thanks to his green blood he can cope with the monster physically, and thanks to his Vulcan mental powers, he can analyze its composition and realize that no phaser fire could have harmed it. Even if the smell of blood does awaken the creature and excite its passion to destroy physically through assault or emotionally through guilt, it can be tamed by the right person.

Kirk throughout has acted on his intuition and has demonstrated how this faculty too is necessary for a starship captain. The crucial moment comes when the cloud, after tasting Spock's green blood, leaves the *Enterprise* and takes off through the universe, leaving no trace nor trail. Although McCoy can only wonder where in the galaxy it can be, instinctively Kirk knows where it has gone. A hunch tells him it is heading for its home on Tycho IV, where Kirk and Captain Garrovick first encountered it. Relying only on this intuition he successfully finds the cloud and destroys it with an antimatter bomb.

Whereas in *The Conscience of the King*, Kirk chooses to wait for evidence which can be verified by anyone, here he relies on the unseen and on associations which well up spontaneously. There he risks the appearance of inaction by not asserting his judgment, here he risks apparent madness by following intuitions no one but himself can verify. Hunches, in fact, aid him often and sometimes, as in *Assignment Earth,* provide the only way he can reach a decision. His instinctive penchant for and understanding of gambling, as in *The Corbomite Manoeuver, The Gamesters of Triskelion,* or *A Taste of Armageddon,* similarly result not from a rational calculation of the odds but an intuitive flash which identifies the right long-shot he should take.

Although all of these faculties emerge time and again in various combinations, these episodes provide examples of individual faculties functioning almost to the exclusion of the others. When the need arises, Kirk can draw on any or all of these functions in a way unequalled by any of his crew. Once again a whole is greater than the sum of its parts and Kirk's human wholeness gives to all of his faculties a unique vitality and adaptability to widely divergent situations.

In *Spectre of the Gun* when Kirk, Spock, and McCoy are gathered at the O.K. Corral awaiting the shoot-out, the wind which is blowing the leaves from the trees affects Kirk's hair only, thereby dramatizing his completeness as a character.

> ... It's yin and yang. *Light is*
> *the left hand of darkness* ...
> how did it go? Light, dark,
> fear, courage. Cold, warmth.
> Female, male. It is yourself.
> Both and one. A shadow on
> snow.
>
> *Ursula LeGuin*

6 Inner Dualities

The mission of the *Enterprise*—to explore new worlds and to extend the frontiers of knowledge —makes the starship the known factor in a perpetually renewed opposition with the unknown of space. The exploration of outer, physical space, however, is simultaneously an exploration of inner human space, which gives shape to the unknown through imagination.

An exhibit at the Air and Space Museum in Washington, D. C. provides an interesting perspective on the relationship between inner and outer space. Starting with a photograph of a man lying on a blanket in Miami, Florida, the camera moves into outer space at the rate of one power of ten every ten seconds. By the time we reach 10^{14} meters, our solar system looks like a star which soon disappears into the vastness of space. As the journey continues, new light clusters appear and grow smaller until at 10^{22} meters even our Milky Way galaxy itself looks like one point of light on the *Enterprise's* viewing screen. After returning to the starting point, we move within the man's body to the interior of one cell of the skin on his hand. By the time we reach 10^{14} meters, we are within the nucleus of a carbon atom, having passed through expanses of "empty" space and "star clusters" of electrons comparable to those we passed through in outer space. In short, there are worlds within comparable to those without, in both space and time.

Besides space, the other essential dimension of *Star Trek* is time. Although the episodes are projected into the future as science fiction, the time they create is the same mythical time there was "in the beginning."

> *in illo tempore*, . . . which has its beginning and end in the human psyche, that spinner of never-ending tales about itself. In that time that never was, we discover the time that always is, for Creation is a never-ending and never-beginning process.[1]

As one departs from the present into either the imagined past or the imaginary future, one enters the world of the psyche.

The world of *Star Trek* returns again and again to map out human nature in terms of three coordinates, three sets of bipolar opposites which we will see in the final chapter can be related to each other as the axes of a cube. Two are physio-

1. June Singer, *Androgyny* (New York: Anchor Books, 1976), pp. 79–80.

logical in origin and hence universally human: sex and age. Male and female, young and old are constant filters for experience for every human who reaches puberty. In addition, *Star Trek* probes another set of opposites imposed by every society in which humans might live: good and evil, the positive and the negative. All three of these polarities provide axes in terms of which we as humans can situate ourselves in order to acquire an awareness of who we are and where we want to go. Through its art, *Star Trek* offers the unselfaware a means of seeing themselves and our world.

Although the oppositions that stem from age, sex, and morality are everyday realities in the world around us, they are often unwelcome when circumstances force an individual to pay serious attention to them. Thus, in *Star Trek* they are often imposed by an etxernal factor which upsets the internal balance on the starship or within its crew. Three episodes which unfold these polarities within the person of Kirk are all triggered by accident or aggression. *The Enemy Within* emerges through a transporter malfunction; *The Deadly Years* are brought on by accidental radiation; *The Turnabout Intruder* is an aggressor. Unwelcome as they may be, these polarities also provide paths to self-knowledge and wholeness. They, too, contribute to Kirk's three-dimensionality and to the human insights implicit in the world of *Star Trek*.

Good/Evil: *The Enemy Within*

Beaming up from planet Alpha 177, Kirk arrives weak and confused only to be followed moments later by a savage and angry double who, because he is unexpected, finds the transporter room empty. Where the positive Kirk finds himself forgetful, confused, and indecisive, the negative Kirk is wildly self-assertive to the point of unprovoked aggression. He demands brandy of McCoy, intrudes on Yeoman Rand, and assaults Technician Fisher. Restrained finally in sick bay, his energies fade; McCoy announces that he is dying without his other half, his regulator. The positive Kirk, on the other hand, realizes with Spock's help that alone, without his other half, he is unfit to command. Although positive Kirk dislikes negative Kirk, the former gradually realizes that the two are really parts of one whole person. Negative Kirk, on the other hand, wants the command for himself but simultaneously fears confrontation with positive Kirk. Although he twice has the opportunity to kill his better half, fear overcomes his aggressive instincts and he flinches.

Spock plays a crucial role in this episode. He first of all helps the positive Kirk fulfill the demands of the captaincy. Positive Kirk, for example, tends to forget that Sulu and other crewmen are freezing to death on the planet below. Spock finally takes over and orders a survival program when positive Kirk proves incapable of coping with the situation. Most important, he helps Kirk make the crucial decision to embrace his other half by reassuring positive Kirk that he can withstand the shock of reunion with his negative side. Spock reminds Kirk and us that he himself is only half human and therefore that he too must bridge an inner split with the help of his mind.

As the transporter was the instrument which brought on the split, so it is the instrument of reunion. The dog-like creature also split in two halves in the process of beaming aboard, dies in the process of rejoining, but Spock convinces Kirk that he must take the risk. The negative Kirk is dying, the positive Kirk steadily losing command control. Spock points out that the "dog" died of shock because it lacked the intellect necessary to cope with its feelings; positive Kirk, however, has the intelligence to survive reunion. Positive Kirk, embracing negative Kirk, enters the transporter, and Spock at the controls brings them back united and alive.

Numerous non-Christian traditions depict opposing principles like those dramatized in *The Enemy Within* as two sides of a single arch which survives precisely because of balance between internal tension: but Judeo-Christian values are very hard on the negative principle, which is identified as devilish and worthy only of eradication. This episode, however, shows how Kirk's negative anti-social tendencies are necessary to his wholeness. Without them, his involvement with others is weakened by apparent indifference and his self-assertion negated by indecision and forgetfulness. As Erich Neumann says,

> Evil, no matter by what cultural canon it be judged, is [as] necessary [a] constituent of individuality as its egoism, its readiness to defend itself or to attack, and lastly as its capacity to mark itself off from the collectivity and to maintain its

"otherness" in the face of the leveling demands of the collectivity.[2]

The Kirk that can command himself and others is the same Kirk that relishes a good fight sometimes and attractive women all the time. Although the reassembled Kirk regrets having seen a part of himself he feels no one should ever see, he is a more integrated person for having done so, for having consciously embraced the negative part of himself which traditional Western values would lead him—and us—to deny. Such is also the source of the effectiveness of this episode as it has been used in psychotherapy.

Youth/Age: *The Deadly Years*

Whereas society generates the polarity between good and evil, our bodies set the context for the next two oppositions. Since aging usually takes place slowly, it is difficult to relate the aged self to the youthful self except in fantasy or imagination. Thoughtful attention to old age is discouraged in a youth- and action-oriented culture like ours. Nonetheless, there is a *Star Trek* episode which takes us into this dimension where there are things to be learned.

In *The Deadly Years*, Kirk, Spock, McCoy, Chekov, and Lieutenant Galway deliver supplies to the colonists on Gamma Hydra IV. There they discover that most of the inhabitants have died from accelerated aging. Not only can they find no reason for this phenomenon, but on returning to

2. Erich Neumann, *Origins and History of Consciousness* (Princeton: Princeton University Press, Bollingen Series XLII, 1954), p. 352–353.

the *Enterprise* they discover that all members of the landing party except Chekov are similarly afflicted. Lieutenant Galway, a woman, dies of old age; Spock ages but because of Vulcan longevity is only affected slowly. McCoy and especially Kirk are soon showing signs of inefficiency, forgetfulness, crankiness, and general senility; Chekov, on the other hand, is unaffected.

Commodore Stocker, a passenger heading for Starbase 10, where he is to take command, convinces Spock that Kirk must be released from duty. Reluctantly Spock does so. In what follows we see Kirk relating to Spock as an elderly father would to a son whom he loved but felt betrayed by. Days earlier they were colleagues; now Kirk and Spock are in different age dimensions.

McCoy and Spock combine to resolve the problem. McCoy has identified radiation poisoning as the cause of the rapid aging, though no standard remedies work until Spock guesses that perhaps Chekov was spared because of the extreme fright he felt when he discovered the first dead body. McCoy then recalls that adrenalin was once, centuries before, a remedy for radiation poisoning. Massive doses of the drug do save the crewmen and restore Kirk to command just in the nick of time.

The Enemy Within showed how the negative Kirk was a necessary part of the captain. It is less clear how the aged Kirk is essential; in fact, he seems to signify the end of Kirk's career. Nonetheless, his presence is essential to the ideal of wholeness implicit in the mission to contact new life forms. By recalling youth and reflecting on old age, one realizes that each individual is really many people. The present is part of a continuum in time along which one can take many forms as well as meet many life forms. An appreciation of the "others" that are potential or probable parts of one's own life trajectory leads to an appreciation of otherness in alien life forms. The mission of the *Enterprise,* which is to make contact with such forms, implies a willingness to move outside of the illusion of one's stability of self in time as well as to explore in space. One aim of the voyage is to transcend egocentricity as much as ethnocentricity.

Male/Female: *Turnabout Intruder*

Nowhere is the illusion of one's stable identity more tenacious than in relation to sex differences. The line between male and female seems at times more impermeable than that between age and youth or between good and evil. Although everyone admits to moments of moral temptation, although everyone knows he or she must age, few will admit to finding room in themselves for their sexual opposite. Kirk, though against his will, does in one episode find a woman within.

The turnabout intruder is Dr. Janice Lester, whom Kirk had known at Star Fleet. Her ambition to be a starship captain has been frustrated by the Star Fleet prejudices which deny such posts to women. Her frustrations turn to hatred of Kirk and lead her to impose a life-energy transfer on him just before she and Kirk are beamed aboard the *Enterprise*. The result is that Kirk's body is inhabited by the psyche of Janice

Lester, who is intent on killing her old body, inhabited by Kirk. She hates not only the Kirk who could repossess his body and his position, but the female body which has been responsible for her lack of promotion to a captaincy. As we see here, the physical body is linked to a social position in the social body defined by Star Fleet.

Once Spock's mind-meld penetrates the body of Janice Lester to contact the captain's psyche within, "Kirk" subjects Spock to court-martial and other members of the crew at last begin to be suspicious. The hysteria displayed by "Kirk" when questioned confirms the suspicions of McCoy and Scott, who recall having seen Kirk drunk and angry but never hysterical. They too are arraigned for courtmartial, and when "Kirk" calls for the death sentence, the entire crew realizes that something is radically wrong. They all refuse obedience. The energy transfer begins to weaken and finally breaks, returning Janice to her own body. Insane with hatred, she attacks Kirk once more but fails to kill him.

While Kirk, the captain, is recognizable in the negative Kirk and the senile Kirk, only Spock can perceive him in the female body of Janice Lester. The others must work from the body of Kirk and the gradual realization that the captain is not within. For the normal crew member and probably the majority of viewers, the idea of a woman in a man's body is hard to accept. It implies a violation of the sacredness of masculinity. It is equally difficult to imagine a man in a woman's body, for that would break the link which binds traditional notions of femininity to the female sex.

Perhaps because of this difficulty, many episodes will turn instead on Kirk's relationship with an alien woman who on closer examination turns out, as we will see in the next chapter, to be a projection of his feminine side, his *anima*, to use Jung's term. What men cannot accept in themselves becomes a script women must act out. Although there can be no female starship captain on the *Enterprise*, whose wholeness could then be a central issue and the turning point of episodes, we will see that *Star Trek* does provide for its women viewers an even richer opportunity for projection. The episodes involving Kirk with an alien woman are so numerous and the implications of women encountering an alien *animus* figure are so important that Chapters 8 and 10 will deal with each subject in turn. Just as Spock in *The Enemy Within* could be more sensitive to Kirk's two selves because of his own dual nature, so we can become more appreciative of others' complexities once we are aware of the aliens we all have within.

To oppose is to maintain.

Ursula LeGuin

7 Outer Oppositions

Where the preceding chapter dealt with the problems of duality within the individual, this one will
consider the same oppositions as they emerge outside the individual. Although the polarity of good
and evil appears to be societal in origin and will
most often be encountered in social terms, we will
see how in the end it merges into universally ap-
plicable principles of the positive and the negative. To trace this evolution, we start with *Mirror,
Mirror*, in which the positive *Enterprise* is discovered to have its negative counterpart. Then in
Day of the Dove the positive Federation, represented by the crew of the *Enterprise*, must cope
with its negative counterpart, the Klingons. In
Let That Be Your Last Battlefield, we move outside the range of Federation politics to encounter

the two remaining inhabitants of the long-dead planet Cheron, who are perpetual antagonists. Finally, in *The Alternative Factor,* we glimpse through a hole in the positive universe its negative counterpart.

As in the episodes dramatizing inner dualities, those in this chapter begin by accident or aggression, as if to imply that duality is in the nature of things and beyond human volition, organization, or control. Thus duality again becomes a universal principle. Although we cannot change it, we can accept and use it constructively rather than destructively.

Positive *Enterprise*/Negative *Enterprise*: Mirror, Mirror

An ion storm approaches the *Enterprise* as Kirk, Uhura, Scott, and McCoy are negotiating with the Halkans for permission to use their dilithium crystals. They must beam aboard even though no agreement has been reached with these people, so peaceful that they refuse their crystals to any party which might use them to cause even a single death. Owing to the storm, however, our friends arrive in a negative *Enterprise* where raw ambition governs and assassination is an accepted means to promotion. Here we learn through the bearded Spock II that the negative *Enterprise* has been ordered to annihilate the peaceful but uncooperative Halkans. Kirk's problem is to prevent such an action as well as to return to the positive *Enterprise*. In attempting to accomplish the first goal, Kirk provokes Spock II into contacting negative Star Fleet, whose orders are to kill Kirk if he does not comply within twelve hours. To return to the positive *Enterprise*, Scott must modify the transporter energy supply without being detected through indicators on the bridge. While he is working in engineering, Uhura is returning Sulu II's earlier sexual advances to distract him from his control panel. Once her mission is accomplished, she leaves as abruptly as she came. Thus the positive *Enterprise* crew members can function positively in the negative world, an ability which ultimately saves them, whereas their negative counterparts cannot function on the positive *Enterprise* where they are confined to the brig.

Spock II warns Kirk of negative Star Fleet's new orders concerning him, but he does not want to kill the captain because he prefers to remain science officer. When Spock II is injured, McCoy risks his safe return to the *Enterprise* in order to treat him. Spock II is amazed that his life has been spared and uses a mind-meld on McCoy to learn the situation. He then accompanies McCoy to the transporter room where Kirk, Scott, and Uhura are waiting. Characteristically loyal even in the mirror universe, he wants Kirk II, his own captain, back and hence runs the transporter himself.

The ion storm which provokes this episode is not the only factor relevant to the problem posed. The nature of the Halkans' excessive pacifism is also relevant to the boundary which separates the negative from the positive. Total pacifism is perhaps also suicide as the negative Spock II so baldly puts it. Their extreme position may also invite an equally extremist response, the total aggressiveness embodied in the negative *Enterprise* and its will to kill.

Whereas Spock's supportive understanding of the situation in *The Enemy Within* provided the way to resolving the problem, his personal integrity is crucial in this episode. He could, if he wanted, kill and replace Kirk, but instead he decides to remain science officer and to restore the integrity of the *Enterprise II*, however negative, by returning the appropriate Kirks to their rightful places. Had Kirk and McCoy not saved Spock II, they could not have returned to their positive *Enterprise*, since it is Spock II who runs the transporter for them. The implication is that had the negative Spock died, the positive one would have suffered a similar fate. As viewers, we are invited to imagine the negative *Enterprise* continuing to shadow the positive counterpart we follow through further episodes. It serves as a reminder of the antithesis which may lurk behind every positive action.

Another glimpse of this polarity occurs in *Whom Gods Destroy* when Garth temporarily assumes the forms of Kirk and Spock; even here the power-grasping motives of Garth betray his identity when he is simulating the bodies of our friends. Spock's and Kirk's positive and assertive stance recurs in *The Savage Curtain*. Here they are confronted by evil as represented by Colonel Green, Genghis Kahn, Kahless, and Zora and survive only because they assert themselves with a directness impossible for their allies, Abraham Lincoln and the Vulcan philosopher, Surak. The episode affirms that the negative side of human nature is also the fearful side, as ready to flee as was the negative Kirk in *The Enemy Within*.

The Good Federation/The Evil Klingon Empire: *Day of the Dove*

In this episode a bodiless being tricks both the Klingons and the crew of the *Enterprise* into believing they have been assaulted by the other. Although the Organian peace treaty still binds both parties to a reluctant truce, they seem eager to accuse each other. The *Enterprise* responds to a distress call from a human colony on a planet, which reveals no trace of habitation or of destruction. While Kirk investigates the surface, the *Enterprise* apparently damages a Klingon ship. Each suspects the other of having developed some new weapon capable of creating these inexplicable situations. Unbeknownst to both parties, the bodiless being infiltrates the *Enterprise* when first the Terrans and then the Klingons beam aboard.

Mysterious events multiply: the *Enterprise* is suddenly and irrevocably sent on a course heading out of the galaxy; a dilithium crystal loses its force; phasers turn into swords; wounds spontaneously heal, leaving the victim physically strong and emotionally bitter. Even Spock is victimized by the racial prejudice of his own colleagues and friends. Spock detects an alien life force on board and observes that its energy level mounts in the presence of hostility. Feeding on antagonism, it has created the situations most likely to keep it well nourished and strong.

Kirk, alerted by Spock, tries to convince

Kang, the Klingon leader, of the truth of his story. During the inevitable fight, Kirk manages to describe the situation to Kang. Fighting will only nourish the being, since neither party will be allowed to die. Heading out of the galaxy, they will be doomed to an eternity of hostility without resolution. Kang sees the being at last and together the Klingons and the crew of the *Enterprise* chase it out into space by means of good humor. Once this has happened, control of the *Enterprise* returns to Kirk, who can now direct its course and use a restored dilithium crystal. Integrity and normal activity are restored through the union of opposites that releases energy once the entity that feeds on the energy of antagonism is gone.

Although the characters do not have the option of eliminating the conflict inherent in opposing forces, they can choose how to deal with it. Understanding and emotional control combine with the will to live which saves both Terrans and Klingons from a suicidal trajectory out of the known world. Given the existence of polarities, a person can choose, once he/she understands the alternatives, to find in them a source of strength rather than a race to destruction.

White/Black: *Let That Be Your Last Battlefield*

One of the more blantantly moralistic of *Star Trek* episodes, this story dramatizes the futile death that awaits those who have let themselves be consumed by hatred. Two men arrive on board the *Enterprise*, Lokai and Bele, each of whom proceeds to plead his cause to the crew and claim the right to kill the other. A vertical line divides each man into a black half and a white half, but their coloring is on opposite sides. As the episode ends, we see Lokai and Bele chasing one another through the maze of the *Enterprise* corridors, dramatizing the endless maze of their antagonism. Though the uninitiated do not at first see the difference between them, they give themselves over to their holy cause and race through the labyrinth which eventually takes them by means of the transporter to a now dead planet. We learn by means of Spock and the sensors that their plant, Cheron, which each of them feels called upon to save, is now uninhabited, its inhabitants having killed each other off in racial wars. Perhaps the call to play messiah invites only destruction.

Matter/Antimatter: *The Alternative Factor*

While Kirk and Spock are exploring an uncharted planet, a bearded man who calls himself Lazarus, calling for help and struggling against an energy field, falls within their view. They take him to sick bay and, on regaining the bridge, learn that there has been an attack by some energy source on the entire galaxy. The *Enterprise* is near the center of this field, which seems to coincide with the nearby planet.

Lazarus tells Kirk of his holy cause, which is to destroy the "devil's own spawn" that has been attacking him. Another mysterious attack on

Lazarus leaves him wounded, and everyone on board is affected by the force of the fight. After tending his patient's wounds, McCoy returns to find no trace of the abrasions. Spock has located a source of radiation coming from nowhere, from a rip in the universe where our laws no longer apply. Lazarus demands dilithium crystals which can counter the force of the attacking devil. Though Kirk denies the request, Lazarus and several crystals disappear.

Spock comes to the rescue: he hypothesizes a second universe paralleling our own; similarly he conceives two Lazaruses, one paranoid, one sane, who are chasing each other. They can exchange worlds through the rip where there is, in effect, a kind of corridor. Should the two meet, however, everything—including both universes—would be destroyed as happens when matter and antimatter meet.

While trying to locate the dilithium crystals Kirk is accidentally catapulted into the alternate world where he meets the rational Lazarus. He learns that the mad Lazarus had accidentally discovered his opposite and become obsessed with his destruction, which would destroy not only both of them, but everything. The only solution lies in trapping the two together in the corridor, which Kirk implements following positive Lazarus' plan. At the agreed time, mad Lazarus is zapped into the corridor and his ship destroyed, preventing his departure. In order to preserve both universes, rational Lazarus voluntarily remains in the corridor to live forever with the mad double chasing him.

In this episode the balanced dynamism extends even beyond the edges of our universe. From this perspective we can encounter the best of the traditional views of the Christian dichotomy between God and the devil. For the universe itself to continue they must continue to coexist, just as the Klingons and the Federation must, just as the two *Enterprises* must, just as each of us must in relation to our own personal demons, our enemies within. Each needs the other half to exist.

Youth/Age: *The Corbomite Manoeuver*

Projected outward, the polarities of age, independent of differences in sex and morality, appear as the relation of old man to young man, father to son. In pure form, uncomplicated by sexual or moral opposites, age opposition occurs only in *The Corbomite Manoeuver* which, although it might seem gimmicky to some, is nonetheless rich in implication, for here appears the only figure who explicitly reveals himself in the course of an episode as both old man and young boy.

The central drama of *The Corbomite Manoeuver* begins as an unexplained cube blocks the path of the *Enterprise*. Spock, aware that they are in uncharted territory, suggests it might be a warning buoy or perhaps something meant to attract—"flypaper." Lieutenant Bailey wants vigorous action to be taken against it. Kirk orders it destroyed. A spherical space ship then appears which has the power to cut all subspace communications from the *Enterprise* and to appear to change size, threatening to engulf the *Enter-*

prise. The head of an old man appears on the viewing screen promising to destroy the ship and crew for having transgressed his territory. Lieutenant Bailey, with whom Kirk has been having trouble, cracks and is sent to his quarters. Drawing on poker strategy, Kirk outwits the Old Man by telling him that if he attacks the starship, the "corbomite" in the hull will return the destructive energy to the sender with equal force. The mirror reflection of destructive force would yield reciprocal destruction, whence a stalemate which can never be broken without risking mutual annihilation.

The Old Man continues to toy with their feelings of terror and potential guilt. He gives them only so many minutes to live but at the last minute nothing happens—he has changed his mind. He invites them to lose control of themselves. Eventually a small ship is sent out to tow them to the Old Man's planet, but the *Enterprise* is able to suddenly veer off and resume its own course. At that moment the towing ship breaks down, and Kirk responds to its distress call, thereby proving his peaceful intentions. On beaming aboard with Bailey, whom, on McCoy's suggestion, Kirk has returned to duty, and McCoy, Kirk discovers that the Old Man is in fact only a fearsome wooden dummy and that a child, Balok, is alone in charge of his fantastic world. Alone and lonely, the child-king wanted company and was merely testing the character of Federation crewmen. The episode ends with Bailey agreeing to stay with Balok to provide companionship in exchange for knowledge of another's world.

Interwoven with the central drama are two

secondary conflicts which echo the clash between authority figures and potentially rebellious "children." Tension on the starship was mounting because of drills Kirk imposed on an already tired crew. During these he seems especially hard on Bailey, at least in the eyes of McCoy, who accuses Kirk of having promoted the young officer too rapidly because he saw in the Lieutenant his own ambitions as a youth. McCoy also asserts his authority as chief medical officer by imposing a diet and chiding the captain for being irritable to his female yeoman. Kirk's grumpy defense is that the *Enterprise* is his woman. Just as McCoy tries to impose fatherly advice on Kirk, the captain emerges as a father-figure himself, especially in relation to Bailey, with whom he is brusquely authoritarian. The harsh old man, Balok, functions as a screen onto which they project their various problems with authority figures, whether as fathers or as sons.

Even before the alien form is encountered, the imbalance on the *Enterprise* centers around Kirk's difficulty in relating to himself as "father" or authority figure. A certain high-handedness prompts his difficulty with Bailey and also his encroachment on potentially hostile territory. He does not heed Spock's warning any more than he heeds Bailey's personal history of the crew's fatigue. The turning point in the episode comes when Kirk, out of compassion and duty, turns back to help the apparently disabled ship of Balok, taking with him McCoy and Bailey, both of whom, from their opposite perspectives, have been his antagonists. He reestablishes positive relations, not only with McCoy and Bailey but also with himself as sentient human rather than authority figure and captain. Simultaneously he opens contact with the Old Man as the boy he really is.

Although the wooden-dummy Balok may seem unfriendly, this episode does not turn on the opposition of good and evil. As we have seen in preceding episodes, evil in *Star Trek* is aggressively and/or wantonly destructive: the negative Kirk's assaults on Yeoman Rand and Technician Fisher, the negative *Enterprise's* reliance on murder, the Klingons' blood lust, Lokai's and Bele's drive for mutual destruction, Lazarus II's compulsion to destroy his opposite. Wooden-dummy Balok, with his appearance of age, represents the accumulation of social prohibition, the perennial thou-shalt-not. In this manner he serves as a catalyst for fears and aggressions; being only a wooden dummy, he cannot be the agent. His force can only come through the imbalance in a person's inner equilibrium.

Our Western heritage presents us with a cosmic drama in which father-god and son are the essential actors; thus any father-son relation which is projected upon the cosmos tends to have a certain religious resonance. In addition, an association of the father with wood recurs not only in Christianity, but also in other images of the father-gods: the erica tree represented Osiris; a fruit tree, Dionysus; the oak, Zeus; the cedar, Tammuz. Yawheh himself says in Hosea 14:8, "I am like a green fir tree. From me thy fruit is found." And just as Adam's fall occurs through eating the fruit of the forbidden tree, other "first men" in mythology fall by breaking off the boughs of a forbidden tree or approaching it too closely. The wooden Balok tries to make Kirk feel that encroaching on Balok's territory is a transgression comparable to the mythological fall and as such deserves similar punishment. Balok plays on guilt before an authority figure by inviting the crew to act rashly and thereby bring about their destruction through fear. Kirk resists, reiterating almost word for word Franklin Delano Roosevelt's dictum that the only thing we have to fear is fear itself.

Many mythological figures have atoned for human guilt through a death that involved a return to the tree in some form: entombment in a tree, crucifixion on a tree. Kirk, however, coolly confronts the Old Man and asserts his freedom at the first possible moment. His return to aid Balok's ship is voluntary, free of guilt and fear. The relationship he establishes is with the child Balok who can relate to him and his crew as an alien but equal and conscious being. In particular, Bailey has learned through Kirk's example that his overly aggressive action, whether turned inward by guilt or outward by hostility, could only destroy one term or the other of the essential opposition which the *Enterprise* sets out to bring together: the known and the unknown. Whereas the mythological father forbids knowledge, which is the fruit of the fall, Balok reveals himself as the child who willingly leads them through the world of his knowledge.

Male/Female: *The Squire of Gothos*

Like *The Corbomite Manoeuver*, this episode provides a unique and instructive example of differentiation based on the polarity of sex without the complication of youth/age or good/evil. At the conclusion of the story we see a male-female pair functioning together as equals in every way. They have no bodies but are represented as lights speaking from the sky; perhaps for this reason they avoid many of the prejudices which color the more common treatments of male and female in *Star Trek*.

The Squire of Gothos begins the episode by abducting Kirk and Sulu on his uncharted planet, whose composition and atmosphere scan as hostile to life. A search party arrives to swell the numbers of unwilling guests of Squire Trelane as he entertains them in styles combining elements from the sixteenth to eighteenth centuries. The crew of the *Enterprise* manage to break out of his realm and rejoin the ship only to find themselves on a collision course with Gothos in outer space. Kirk beams down and is subjected to a trial, with the Squire playing the elderly judge. Kirk challenges Trelane to vary the monotony of a simple death by proposing a fox hunt game instead of an execution, though Kirk inevitably loses through Trelane's psionic powers. At the crucial moment twin lights appear as cosmic parents and apologize for their son's mischief. They had not realized the vulnerability of the Terrans and will punish their son by not letting him toy with any more planets.

Although Balok's trial of the *Enterprise* prefigures Trelane's trial of Kirk, the former had mythical resonance whereas the latter does not. Balok became the guide who could lead others through the world of his knowledge, but Trelane emerges as simply the naughty boy playing with his planetary erector set. Even the male-female luminous deities remain too much a *divinitas ex machina* to enrich the episode. Nonetheless the implication is there that a large dimension exists where sexual duality finds a resolution.

Our culture has been slower to come to terms with sexual polarity than with either of the two axes prominent in *Star Trek*. We can easily accept the polarities of age and youth as simply defining two ends of one continuum. Acceptance of the idea of gradations in evil is also built into the legal code with its variety of "appropriate" punishments for crimes of differing seriousness. Thus the linking of these polarities on a social or universal scale has a precedent in our commonly accepted experience. The possibility of seeing sexual differences as belonging to a common continuum is, however, a recent phenomenon. Scientific inquiry has in fact only begun to call our attention to the difficulty of defining absolute categories of sexual difference. We are perhaps coming to realize that sexual distinctions are merely the poles of a continuum which can be characterized in a variety of ways: chromosomal hormonal balance, genital structure, perhaps even psychological characteristics.

If, as Claude Lévi-Strauss asserts, myth is an act of faith in a science yet unborn, we can perhaps glimpse in myths and rituals of society a version of truths science has yet to unravel. Some people have even seen the androgyne, the being who combines both sexes, in the roots of our Western tradition. Adam himself is represented in early rabbinical commentary as androgynous; the *Bereshit rabba* sees Adam and Eve as being created back to back, joined at the shoulders until Yahweh divided them in two with an axe. Another commentary describes Adam as a man on one side, a woman on the other before Yahweh divided them into two halves. From this view, as June Singer points out, earthly Adam was simply a reflection of the celestial two-sexed archetype; both heaven and earth were androgynous. The descendants of Adam and Eve, then, can find their true wholeness in joining the male *and* female elements which are necessarily part of every person. "Spiritual perfection consists precisely in rediscovering within oneself this androgynous nature."[1] Having emerged from a primeval androgyne into a fallen and imperfect state, we need to regain the lost paradise of integrity.

In some societies, recognition of one's sexual opposite is prerequisite for admission into the adult community. Among the Masai of Africa, for example, boys undergoing puberty rites must dress up as girls; in the Sotho tribe of South Africa girls must dress up as men before becoming full adult community members. Mircea Eliade offers an explanation of the psychic significance of such rituals:

> The novice has a better chance of attaining to a particular mode of being—for example, becoming a man, a woman—if he first symbolically becomes a totality. For mythical thought, a particular mode of being is necessarily preceded by a *total* mode of being. The androgyne is considered

1. *Androgyny*, p. 77.

superior to the two sexes just because it incarnates totality and hence perfection.[2]

Plato hypothesized an original creation including a whole man, a whole woman, and an androgyne. These entities were split and dispersed among humankind, yielding three basic human types: men so masculine in orientation that they have no interest in women, women so exclusively feminine that they ignore men, and mixed individuals (men who seek out women, women attracted to men). If human history is any test of the frequency of the three ideal types in humankind, then the mixed individuals descended from the original androgyne certainly seem to predominate.

The conception of the androgyne, then, is available in primitive societies and in the cultural roots of our Western tradition, but it seems as peripheral to the categories of our everyday existence as the masculine-feminine deity in *The Squire of Gothos* is to the main events of the episode. An androgynous entity, in fact, is easier to conceive the less it is embodied. The two equal but sexually differentiated lights have voices but no corporeal appearance. Once sexual differences are embodied, the situation changes considerably, as we shall see in the following chapter.

2. Mircea Eliade, *Birth and Rebirth: The Religious Meanings of Initiation in Human Culture* (New York, Harper & Brothers, 1958), p. 26.

> The trouble about women is
> that they must always go on
> trying to adapt themselves to
> men's theories of women.
>
> *D. H. Lawrence*

8 The Disposable Female

In almost every episode we have a different female guest star, which usually guarantees that the character she portrays is alien and disposable. Most often she dies, disappears, or remains at the service of a father-figure, if not her actual father. Fatherhood as portrayed in the world of *Star Trek* expands to match the importance of fatherhood in our patriarchal society. If in our everyday experience the father creates the child's social world by means of his name, job, and status, in the world of *Star Trek* some fathers can single-handedly create their children: they can make androids or materialize thoughts, neither of which can achieve existence independent of their masculine makers. Even when the disposable female is not responsible to a father-figure, she serves the needs of some other male, as we see in the following episode.

The Insubstantial *Anima: Shore Leave*

On a planet where Kirk hopes the crew can enjoy rest and recreation, activities associated with home, a landing party discovers an ideal earth-like atmosphere. Soon, however, strange events take place. McCoy sees the white rabbit from *Alice in Wonderland*; Sulu finds the old-earth pistol he has always wanted. Kirk first encounters Finnegan, a former fellow student at the Space-Academy who used to taunt him. A knock-down, drag-out fight ensues as Kirk has his first chance to work off his long-time grudge against Finnegan.

The mysterious encounters gain in danger and seriousness when Sulu is attacked by a Samurai and another crewman is subjected to a World War Two-style strafing he has imagined vividly since his youth. McCoy accompanies a female crew member who puts on her ideal medieval dress after it miraculously appears on a bush. A medieval knight threatens to run McCoy down with a lance, but he pays no heed since he is sure that hallucinations can do no harm. He is flattened and apparently killed.

McCoy's death reunites the crew in examining the knight, whom Kirk has killed with Sulu's gun. Spock discovers that our medieval avatar is in fact made entirely of cellulose (as is all of the vegetation). While they crowd around the knight, McCoy disappears; when they look for him, the knight disappears. An old man dressed as a wizard appears as if from nowhere; Kirk is challenging him angrily over the death and disappearance of McCoy when the latter appears with playboy bunnies on each arm. The wizard explains that he creates all these figures, which are simply cellulose projections of the thoughts and desires of each individual. The results can be fearsome or pleasant depending on the person's inner state. Once they know the rules of the game, the crew members can concentrate on imagining their fondest wishes and watch them come true.

One theme already dealt with reappears here, the father as tree. The entire planet and all of its inhabitants are cellulose, that is, made up of the essential component of wood. But this father-figure is benevolent: the wizard assures them that the planet is there *for* them, for their rest and recreation.

The single most important figure among the fantasy embodiments created by the wizard is Ruth, Kirk's former love and the final factor which convinces him to accept this remarkable form of rest and recreation for the crew as a whole. Ruth appears first after Kirk savors the beauty of a red flower, which he breaks off and smells. Evidently, the flower brings Ruth to his mind, because she instantly appears and begins to walk toward him. Kirk is interrupted as they meet and she vanishes from the television screen as she does from his mind, only to reappear as he is making up his mind about accepting the planet's "hospitality."

By the definitions of the planet, Ruth is insubstantial, simply a perfect cellulose copy of the woman Kirk remembers and still loves. However beautiful, she remains an embodied figment of his imagination without an independent existence of her own. If Kirk should cease to think of her, she would presumably just disappear. Hence, she is clearly a projection of his *anima,* the internalized image of ideal femininity he carries inside him. Through reencountering this ideal in the "flesh," Kirk can begin to reunite with his inner self, recharge his batteries, find rest, and re-creation. Kirk, in fact, repeatedly finds something of Ruth-*anima* in every woman he loves, though most have more physical substance than Ruth in this episode.

The Android Anima: Requiem for Methuselah

Here the mission is not rest and recreation but recovery from illness, though once again the motivating factor is the drive to correct an imbalance within the *Enterprise.* The crew of the starship is suffering from Rigellian fever for which the only antidote is ryetalyn. In search of it on an apparently uninhabited planet, Kirk, Spock, and McCoy discover a Mr. Fint, who, although at first hostile, seems to be moved by the plight of a crew stricken by a disease as deadly as bubonic plague. He sends his robot out to collect the needed substance and invites the trio into his most unusual home. Spock is immediately impressed with his art collection and with the Brahms score on the piano, which is still in the process of being written. We also make the acquaintance of his "daughter" Reena, whom he encourages to get acquainted with Kirk. The two dance together, walk and talk together; finally they kiss, provoking an attack by Flint's robot, programmed to protect Reena.

In the conversation which follows between Reena and Flint, we see signs that feelings of independence are emerging in Reena. She does not want to be protected, even though Flint protests that in general such protection and programming have provided the good life that they have. As Flint is having his troubles with Reena, so McCoy has problems with the robot's lab work. The ryetalyn it supplies is impure and unusable. In order to oversee the processing of a second sample, McCoy and the others search out the laboratory area only to find at least 16 androids covered with sheets, and all labeled *Reena*. Flint has gradually been perfecting his dream girl up to the present model, which lacks only emotion to make her human.

Mr. Flint is in fact as old as Methuselah. Endowed with spontaneous cell regeneration, Flint is over six thousand years old and has been Da Vinci as well as Brahms and many others. He has remained and outlived scores of earth women, resulting in cumulative and intolerable loneliness. Although it meant the end of his immortality, he left earth for this planet, where the supply of ryetalyn could permit him to make himself a perfect companion. He not only made Reena beautiful but programmed her with encyclopedic knowledge and high intellectual ability. Her only lack is the human emotion which could give Flint the love he craves. He despairs of inspiring an android with emotion until Kirk arrives. Flint's plan is that Kirk will rouse Reena to feeling, but then withdraw so that Reena will love only Flint. He discovers that feelings once awakened are not easily susceptible to control.

Reena, who has often been drawn to the lab as a place for meditation or pondering vague questions she cannot quite formulate, overhears Kirk and Flint arguing and discovers the truth about her origins. Kirk challenges her to claim her rightful freedom, to leave this planet, and enjoy an independent human life, now that her feelings are alive. He implies that she can join him on his voyages into space. Flint, however, claims allegiance as her creator to whom she owes everything, to whom she can turn for everything she needs. As a father he is benevolent, yet he needs her to be dependent on him and under his control. When Kirk and Flint fight, Reena, realizing that she is the cause, dies. Having only recently known emotion, she encounters the whole range of feelings before knowing how to cope with them, and the shock destroys her.

Being an android, Reena is more substantial than the materialized fantasies we encounter in *Shore Leave*. Nonetheless, she is created by a man to embody a projection of part of himself to help him overcome solitude and feel himself a completed individual. Existing within a context to acknowledged illusion, Ruth was never considered a potential companion for Kirk once he returned to the *Enterprise*. Reena's physical existence, on the other hand, does not depend on the continued presence of Flint. Theoretically she could leave her planet, though the possibility overstrains her emotional resources. Forced to choose between the father who has given her existence and the lover who has inspired her humanity, she dies. She cannot assert herself to establish an independent identity.

As we saw in *The Enemy Within*, the positive Kirk who lacked his negative side was also unable to assert himself and fulfill his role as captain. Reena is in an analogous situation. Flint in his desire to make the perfect companion protected her from all of those troublesome aspects of the "outside" world. Although Reena has extraordinary mental powers, she cannot cope with aggression. Not having been exposed to the negative aspects of life, she cannot assert herself independently. Lacking experience with the negative, she cannot join the on-going *Enterprise*. Without access to the polarities which give three-dimensionality to existence, Reena remains a projection of the male psyche, dependent on the masculine. She is another *anima* figure in the tradition of mermaids and other half-human half-alien females who are so appealing to male fantasy because they are projections of the feminine in men.

The Daughter *Anima: The Mark of Gideon*

The imbalance which motivates this episode is not on the *Enterprise*, but on the planet Gideon. Although it is an apparently idyllic place where there is no disease, the planet has resisted diplomatic contacts with the Federation. When Kirk beams down to parley, he disappears into an alternate starship, a perfect replica in which he finds himself alone with Odona, the beautiful daughter of Hodin, the leader of Gideon. Kirk learns through her that, although free of disease, Gideon is far from idyllic; superb health combined with affirmative attitudes toward life such that contraception and abortion are forbidden has created an over-populated hell where death would be merciful. People would riot for the solitude she can now enjoy with Kirk.

Kirk's pleasure with Odona is disturbed by the fact that he cannot remember several minutes during the transfer. Eventually, after Odona becomes ill, the Gideons reveal themselves and their plot: they have taken a blood sample from his arm during these few minutes and injected it in Odona so that she will become infected with choriomeningitis, a disease Kirk has survived. When she leaves the model spaceship, she will then infect others and by reintroducing death, reestablish the necessary balance between people and space. Her death is to be a symbol to the others that will help reestablish the value of dying. The Gideons also want to keep Kirk as a continuing agent of infection. With Spock's intervention and McCoy's help, Kirk saves Odona so that her blood can then be used instead of his to infect Gideons with disease. She is grateful to Kirk for saving her and happy to serve as her father's virus bank.

Although Odona is a "normal daughter" and Hodin her "real father," she continues to function as did Ruth and Reena. She has little existence or identity apart from what the father has created. Although Odona is neither an android nor an embodied fantasy, an aura of "otherness" is created by means of the alternate, unreal *Enter-*

prise. Kirk and Odona fall in love in a starship that is at once familiar and different. Everything is where it ought to be, but the crew is missing and the captain is unable to make anything work. They are in an unreal space which they must leave in order to return to reality.

Although Odona shows no rebelliousness at serving as a function of the masculine will, a quick look at *Wink of an Eye* provides an interesting parallel which demonstrates how differently we feel when Kirk is subject, for a time, to the will of a female. On the Scalosian planet the men have been rendered sterile through radiation resulting from a volcanic eruption. To have children, the Scalosian queen, Deela, must choose a human male after rendering him fit for life on Scalos by accelerating his life processes to such a rate that humans wear out rapidly. Deela is, of course, very beautiful and becomes fond of Kirk as her temporary male. She asks her men to be very careful since she does not like damaged goods. In this situation Kirk is the disposable male. Needless to say, he is not pleased with the prospect of becoming an animated sperm bank and with Spock's help finds an escape. The Scalosians will cease to exist but Kirk points out very clearly that their problems lie within themselves and that they have no right to demand that others live as kept men and die prematurely so that the Scalosian race and way of life can continue. He will defend himself and his crew from the disposability—though that seems to be the normal condition of the various females from other times and spaces he encounters in episode after episode. Kirk has incorporated the negative self that can permit assertiveness; however, few women have done so. As we see in *The Lights of Zetar* women in *Star Trek* are more susceptible to suggestion, less able than men to affirm an independent identity.

The imbalances provoking these episodes have all involved a Mother Nature in some way out of equilibrium. *Shore Leave* must be taken to restore a tired crew through rest and recreation; ryetalyn is needed to restore the physical health of the crew; on Gideon disease is needed to reestablish population balance on a planet as overrun with people as the *Enterprise* was with tribbles (*Trouble with Tribbles*); a natural catastrophe led to sterility on Scalos, as it had on Talus IV.

Just as the circular portion of the starship, which carries and cares for the crew, is manmade, so nature on these various planets must be corrected if not created by men. Symbolically, then, although male characters encounter father-figures, the female figures are missing a mother. There is only the male wizard in *Shore Leave*, who is responsible for the materialized fantasies; Flint, alone, creates Reena; Hodin makes no mention of the woman who presumably bore Odona and could presumably nurture her and defend her right to live. The women in these episodes are functions of the father, projections of the masculine psyche; they are *anima* images and disposable in so far as they cannot enjoy an independent existence. Deela simply reverses the terms without resolving the issue, as she too proves disposable.

The Priestess *Anima: The Paradise Syndrome*

On a mission to save a planet which is on a collision course with an asteroid, Kirk, Spock, and McCoy discover that the planet is much like earth during an idyllic time when the American Indians lived undisturbed and peaceful. Accidentally, Kirk falls into an obelisk marked with strange hieroglyphs. Inside the obelisk Kirk happens to trigger an energy field which wipes his memory clean. The otherness of the dimension he enters is signaled by the squaring of his usually pointed sideburns. On emerging from the obelisk he is taken by the tribe's priestess to be the god they are awaiting to save them from the storms and destruction which accompany the approach of asteroids.

The priestess, Miramanee, takes Kirk to her father, the chief of the tribe, and to the current medicine man who, thanks to his father's possessiveness of his secrets, does not know how to activate the obelisk which could divert asteroids. Kirk, by successfully applying artificial respiration to a young boy who has drowned, convinces them that he is indeed a god. Miramanee is given Kirk in marriage, and the two share a short but idyllic life together. Just existing and loving, Kirk is happier than he has ever been before, though he shows his creative nature by inventing indoor lighting and devising a system for irrigation which should improve their agricultural output.

The storms which announce imminent collision with the asteroid begin. Kirk, who cannot remember anything about the obelisk, is attacked as a fraud along with Miramanee. Spock arrives as they are being stoned and, having deciphered the hieroglyphs in the interim, activates the obelisk to divert the asteroid. Thanks to him, the god-like activity is accomplished. And thanks to him, Kirk's memory is restored by means of the mind-meld, though Miramanee dies of the wounds inflicted by her fellow tribesmen.

Although Miramanee has an independent physical existence, she is the chief's daughter, predestined to be the wife of the medicine man. By tribal tradition she has a social existence circumscribed by the men who govern the tribe. To her father she is the link with the medicine man and thus with the ancient laws for tribal survival. To the medicine man she is the prize he earns for accepting his responsibilities. In the long run, her life is ground to pieces by the social machinery of her tribe. For Kirk she is *anima*, the ideal love, but Kirk can love her only when he is not himself, having lost his memory and even the certainty of his name. His emotional fulfillment with Miramanee takes place in the freedom of an idyllic fantasy world which he must leave in order to resume his identity as starship captain. Miramanee, too, has no mother to defend her existence; she, too, is disposable.

The Maternal Anima:
The City on the Edge of Forever

McCoy's accidental overdose of a stimulant induces temporary madness, during which he beams down and leaps through a womb-like time portal. Spock and Kirk must follow if they are to retrieve their friend. On the other side they find themselves in New York City as it was in the 1930s. They soon meet Edith Keeler, a daughter who has rejected her wealthy father to help the poor by running a settlement house. Again the mother-figure is absent except for the strong maternal instincts of Edith. Her "home" is a mission for the needy; her chief mission in life is the motherly ideal of peace in the world. Kirk and Spock find shelter in her home, and Kirk finds in her a woman of his dreams. While Spock tries to create a communication device, Kirk courts Edith.

Spock finally succeeds and learns that from their present vantage point, there are two historical options open to them. The option which leads to the world that they know, the world of the *Enterprise,* necessitates Edith's death. If she should live, she would organize a peace movement so powerful that the entry of the United States into the Second World War would be delayed long enough for Hitler to win. The course of history would be so changed that neither the Federation nor the *Enterprise* would ever exist. On the other hand, if the *Enterprise* is to remain in its future existence, Edith must be run down by a car, symbolizing, in effect, the on-going momentum of history. Torn between his responsibility to the history of the future (which is the distant past to the *Enterprise* world) and his happy love with Edith, Kirk leaves the home on a date with her. The crucial moment comes as Kirk sees McCoy, still in his starship uniform, and rushes across the street to rejoin his friend.

Edith, transfixed by seeing the strange reunion, fails to notice the car that is about to hit her. Kirk sees the coming catastrophe, but Spock, reminding Kirk of what is at stake, prevents him from saving her life. Edith Keeler, too, must die.

As the death of Miramanee is the price for the continuation of the tribe, so the death of Edith guarantees the continuity of history on which the existence of the *Enterprise* depends. Her pacifism, if she were alive to promote it, would neutralize a national aggressiveness which seems necessary. To fail to fight would destroy the balanced opposition which releases energy. Nazism would have ruled the world and would not have risked its monopoly of power by reaching out to the unknown.

This episode has great psychological resonance. The attack of insanity which McCoy suffers, triggering the leap through the time portal, symbolizes the madness of returning to the past or of wanting to change one's past. To move into the past, or to want the past to have been other than it was, is to want to cease to exist as the person one is. Edith Keeler as the mother idealized from the past, as the embodiment of that male dream of an impossible all-encompassing hospitality, is as deadly as a mermaid. Just as the tolerance she would extend to the Nazis would annihilate the world as we know it, so on the personal level loving kindness which smothers all aggressiveness would mean the end of our lives as we know them. She is an *anima*-figure, a fantasy woman created by men in response to their dreams of infinite rest and re-creation. To try to live in her territory is a fatal madness. As fantasy she by definition cannot live side by side with men in a world considerably less than ideal. Either her ideal nature must be left behind or existence itself is threatened.

This episode, though its implications appear elsewhere in *Star Trek,* is particularly important because of its wide popularity. Not only did it earn a Hugo award for the writer who officially received credit for it, Harlan Ellison, but also this has been the most widely sold script since Lincoln Enterprises began making all scripts available. This popular appeal indicates how much resonance the story generates, a resonance which is evidence for its psychic profundity even for viewers who are not conscious of just why it appeals to them.

These disposable *anima*-women function as men's fantasies. As ideals projected by the male psyche, they are forever cut off from those negative characteristics which, as we saw in *The Enemy Within,* can give the three-dimensionality and the assertiveness necessary to be captain of oneself. They are cut off from the three bipolar axes to knowledge treated earlier. They have no mothers who could defend their right to live or who could provide the possibility of seeing themselves in the dimension of age. As idealized fantasies, they cannot encounter their opposites along the scale of good and evil. Female figures conceived as embodiments of male fantasies, they cannot encounter men on the axis of sex on an equal and potentially maturing basis.

One important implication of this phenomenon can be seen in *Wolf in the Fold.* In this episode, Jack the Ripper assumes an eternal dimension as the prototypical rapist-murderer who becomes embodied in a succession of males around the galaxy. His victims are women who, in Spock's analysis, fall into this role through their greater susceptibility to fear. Unable to integrate their assertiveness, they project this side of themselves outward onto others and thus become the victims of the aggressiveness they cannot acknowledge with themselves. The evil spirit of the murderer so depends on the food of fear that without this support in the surrounding people, it dies. Men, insofar as they are motivated by intellect and sensation, are better able to control their feelings and hence provide less appealing fare than the traditional emotional-intuitive female. The *anima*-woman as the ideal of male fantasies is also the ideal victim.

One episode reveals explicitly the difference between *anima*-figures and believably real women. In *Mudd's Women*, Harry Mudd, the galactic con man, beams aboard the *Enterprise* with three women whose sexual attractiveness affects the entire crew. Mudd trades in women, in this case selling them to isolated miners. He attributes their sex appeal to his love crystals, which turn women who feel themselves to be unattractive into sex magnets. As the episode evolves, we see that the crystals are fake and that the magic they work is psychological in origin. Belief in the crystals allows the women to believe in their desirability, a faith which actually transforms their appearance for a time into the pin-up beauties all men seem to long for. One miner feels gypped when he encounters his woman "as she really is." She, through the acceptance she feels with Kirk, has chosen to risk living with reality to reveal Mudd's trickery. She learns that she can relate to her man more realistically as a helpmate who, though no longer a pure *anima* fantasy, still functions as an ancillary to men. Spock compares her helpmate characteristics, however, with the dilithium crystals which run the ship and which become blackened with overuse and age. He alone is sorry for them, implying that they have in some way been used and abused.

A woman *is* her mother.
That's the main thing.

Anne Sexton

9 The Monstrous Mother

So far we have identified the feminine in several contexts: first as embodied in the *Enterprise* itself, then as dramatized in the feminine faculties of sensation and intuition prominent in McCoy, then in disembodied forms as the shapeless unknown of space penetrated by the *Enterprise*, and then as *anima*, primarily in the alien women temporarily tied to Kirk. Especially in the character of Edith Keeler, we saw how the *anima* could overlap with the mother figure: both exist in the past as symbols of peace and unlimited hospitality as a kind of edenic paradisal dream. The idea of the feminine, in fact, seems to evolve from the universal human experience of Mother, that vast reservoir of unconscious preexistence

[143]

from which we all emerge into being. "She" remains as a backdrop which counterpoints the changing consciousness of growing beings just as she is also the matrix of eternal space and darkness through which the *Enterprise* continues to explore.

Paradoxically, the idea of the nothingness that is space-Mother can appear embodied as a separate entity that has at least minimal form, for example, that of a gaseous cloud. Such entities embody projected fears of being lost in space, in nothingness, in unconsciousness. Thus in several episodes which carry the *Enterprise* beyond the boundary of the galaxy, returning to recognizable coordinates becomes an immediate necessity. To fail to do so would be to remain forever lost, just as Kirk fears would happen—on the psychic level —if he should lose command of himself on the *Enterprise*. Being alone in a universe all to oneself, as Kirk is in *The Tholian Web*, is a frightening equivalent to insanity, to being lost in the "primary mother-matter," the unknown, the unconscious.

In the world of *Star Trek*, this fear is sometimes projected as an ill-defined creature whose chief life function is to swallow up and annihilate conscious life forms. Such creatures embody a human terror in the face of the unknowable as old as the Hindu Mother-goddess Kali, who in one of her aspects is the prototype of the omnivorous Mother.

> Kali is a protective mother to those who prostrate themselves before her in abject supplication, but . . . is depicted also as a sort of demon with

gnashing teeth, who stands on top of her male adversary, cuts off his head, and drinks his blood.[1]

She also eats her own children. She is ravenous motherhood that is as all-devouring as the ideal Garden is all-nourishing. The devouring Mother from time to time threatens the *Enterprise* as well.

The Omnivorous Mother: The Immunity Syndrome

While the *Enterprise* is once again on its way to rest and recreation, Spock is seized by the knowledge that the starship *Intrepid* with four hundred Vulcans aboard has just ceased to exist. Star Fleet then reports having lost contact with the Gamma 7A star system and the *Intrepid*, which had been in the area. As the *Enterprise* goes to investigate, the crew members become nervous, weak, and irritable. They are approaching a blackness, an area of total darkness which does not show up on the sensors since it is non-existence. Painful sonic waves attack their ears, and the stars fade from the viewing screen as the ship crosses into the blackness. The ship loses power, and McCoy must administer stimulants to counter a similar loss of energy affecting everyone on board.

A sudden shock wave indicates they are in a new zone where normal laws are reversed: to resist the pull which is drawing them to the center

1. Wolfgang Lederer, *The Fear of Women* (London & New York: Grune & Stratton, 1968), p. 137.

of the dark, they must put the engine on full forward, not reverse. At last the sensors detect a blob that is eleven thousand miles long and varying between two and three thousand miles in thickness. The outside is covered with space debris, but the inside is living protoplasm which feeds on energy of any sort. Like a giant space amoeba, it does nothing but engulf and eat.

Spock heads into the creature in a shuttlecraft on what all feel to be a suicide mission. He observes that reproduction is beginning: the chromosomes are all lined up for mitosis, which would result in two such creatures devouring the stuff of the universe. Because of power loss, Spock cannot tell Kirk how to kill the creature, but the captain manages to solve the problem on his own. He takes the *Enterprise* through the blob's outer membrane to destroy it with an antimatter bomb in its nucleus. The explosion miraculously preserves both Spock and the starship; the death of the creature restores the stars and space to normal. The creature acted as a threatening virus in the world of the *Enterprise*, and the starship proved a fatal virus in its world.

The creature's "femininity" is evident first of all in its darkness, turned aggressive as it devours light and energy. Also, it is made up of minimally living matter, protoplasm, which seeks only to reproduce itself. Its hostility as devouring mother has special significance in relation to its Vulcan victims, for the Vulcans have lived in peace for eons, partly because they have special capacities for communicating with the unknown, the unconscious, and the inarticulate. The disaster of the starship *Intrepid* was the overwhelming of extraordinary consciousness by dull proto-plasm. The deaths of the four hundred Vulcans do contribute to the omnivorous Mother's destruction, however, since her "meal" on the *Intrepid* blunted her hunger enough so that the *Enterprise* could conserve power sufficient to carry out the kill.

The Man-Made Mother: The Doomsday Machine

Here we have an analogous creature, although it does have a shape: a gigantic open-mouthed cone so energy-hungry that it devours starships and solar systems in its maw. It has reduced the Federation starship *Constellation* to a derelict which harbors only its now mad captain, Matt. He is brought to the *Enterprise* while Kirk stays on the disabled ship to prepare it for towing.

On the *Enterprise* Matt wants to take over and launch a suicidal revenge attack on the monster. Spock must struggle for his rightful place as commanding officer in Kirk's absence. Finally Matt pursues his suicide mission by himself in a shuttlecraft and thereby suggests to Kirk how the wreckage of the *Constellation* can be used as a time bomb to blow up the monster from inside. Kirk and Spock together accomplish this, though Spock gets Kirk back just in the nick of time.

Several themes recur here: the energy hunger, the omnivorousness of blind matter pursuing its instinctual course, the human suicide mission to subdue it, the final destruction which can only come from within. In this case, however, there is no reproduction, for this monster is, according to Spock's analysis, an artificial war machine designed to bluff the opponent into compliance but now somehow gone wild. Although Spock's hypothesis seems simply like good scientific explanation on the surface, it has a further implication. Insofar as Western culture has focused most of its attention on the image of the Good or idealized Mother, it has ignored the Bad Mother to a considerable extent. The masculine domination of our culture over centuries has favored the male fantasies not only of *anima* lovers but also of impossibly pure and positive, sometimes even virgin, Mothers. The negative, devouring Mother does not disappear but takes covert revenge through disrupting human creations which presume to deny her existence. Whereas the amoeba-blob was a natural phenomenon, the doomsday machine is man-made. Whereas the Dark Mother can appear in natural form, she can also, if men try to suppress awareness of her existence, re-emerge through corrupting man's own constructions. Her presence might even be inferred behind the destructive fertility of a planet like Gideon.

The Vampire Mother: *Obsession*

Here we encounter another creature reminiscent of the negative Mother. The gaseous cloud, like the cosmic amoeba, can only consume, though its tastes have become more precise: it eats the iron from human hemoglobin and has intelligence of a rudimentary sort. Spock in his rationality sees it as simply a being whose dietary habits have unfortunate consequences for humans. Kirk, however, is stirred by intuitions and doubts. When the cloud turns to invade the *Enterprise*, Kirk is sure that its intelligence is malevolent. Since its actions are evil rather than simply instinctive, he feel compelled to pursue it, as we saw in Chapter 5. Its destruction clears the galaxy, for the time being, of yet another demonic Mother-creature.

The Protective Mother: The Devil in the Dark

The episode opens with a distress call: a mining colony has discovered both an extraordinary lode and a monster which has already destroyed several workers. For work to continue, for the colony even to survive, the monster must be found and stopped.

As Kirk is talking to the man in charge of the colony, Spock notices some perfectly round silicon spheres; his questions about them are dismissed as irrelevant, but nonetheless he wishes to begin his search on the level where they were found. Just as the crew of the *Enterprise* is about to begin their work, "it" attacks, nearly destroying the pump for circulating air. Its means of attack is to burn and dissolve all that it touches. In spite of Spock's protests that it might be a unique specimen, Kirk orders his men to shoot to kill.

Down in the mining tunnels, Spock and Kirk are examining the stone when suddenly Spock's tricorder readings indicate that some of the silicon is alive. Shortly thereafter a crewman is dissolved. Kirk and Spock arrive just as the monster is leaving and Kirk wounds it with phaser fire. He reiterates the warning that his men should be doubly cautious because wounded creatures are doubly vicious. Kirk and Spock find a double tunnel and decide to separate so that each can explore one branch of it.

Partway into his tunnel Kirk meets *it*. Whereas he had warned his men to shoot to kill, he himself becomes curious and, while keeping it covered with his phaser, attempts talking with it. Now it is Spock who warns him to shoot to kill. On arriving Spock notices more silicon nodules. Kirk suggests that for a wounded creature it is behaving very unusually and asks Spock to do a mind-meld. Spock is at first overcome by the creature's pain, but it too has been touched by the contact and burns into the floor of the tunnel "NO KILL I." While McCoy is trying to heal the creature by means of silicon cement beamed down from the *Enterprise,* Spock learns that it is a horta, the sole surviving member of a race that every 50,000 years dies off, leaving only its eggs and one adult female to care for them. The miners had been breaking the silicon nodules that assure the continuation of the species. Kirk saves the creature from an onslaught of angry miners and works out a *modus vivendi.* They will respect the needs of the horta, who along with the babies about to hatch will eat rock tunnels to help the miners locate and remove the minerals valuable to the Federation.

In the image of the horta we have a beautifully rich symbolism. She is much more than the simple hungry mother. Her appetite can function for others as well as herself. She is sufficiently intelligent to be considerate of her children's existence, to respond reasonably to the actions of others, to control her pain, and finally to win the respect of Spock. Spock's Vulcan powers of mind have permitted opening direct communication with a radically alien life form. His mind-meld made comprehensible what would otherwise have remained unknown and hence feared.

In addition, when we pursue the archetypal resonance of the horta, we can see her as an avatar of the medieval philosopher's stone. Like the philosopher's stone, the horta is "a stone and not a stone, a stone of great virtue."[2] In alchemy texts this stone is described as guarded by a poisonous dragon, which is composed of the same material as the stone. To get beyond the guard and find the stone, one must visit the inner parts of the earth and approach it with a moral rectitude comparable to that of Spock, the Vulcan who does not lie. One medieval writer even describes what could have been the horta's eggs: "The material of the stone, unknown to the profane, is a black ball with which the children play but which men disregard and tread upon."[3] The philosopher's stone represents the state of spiritual purity which one must obtain in order to see it for what it is. Kirk and Spock together succeed in doing so and thereby save the horta from extinction and the miners from bankruptcy and/or destruction.

In this episode the mother-figure as matter

2. Grillot de Givry, *Witchcraft Magic, and Alchemy* (Boston: Houghton, Mifflin and Co., 1931), p. 366.
3. Grillot de Givry, p. 361.

in space has been consolidated into the very dense *prima materia* of Earth Mother. Where in space she was too alien, too purely instinctual, too single-mindedly hungry for anything but destruction, here she acquires an intelligence which recognizes the Other as deserving of life space and existence. The world is no longer undifferentiated dinner. Although eating is still the horta's main way of relating to the world, she manages to make it expressive. She eats those who destroy her children in order to relieve her rage and to stop the predators. Though some creatures are too hopelessly alien for peaceful coexistence and sometimes must be destroyed or returned to their own kind (as was the case with Charlie X), the horta symbolizes the success of the *Enterprise's* mission. Through the mediation of Spock, she becomes a welcome member of an expanded society of living beings.

The Nurturing Mother: *Metamorphosis*

Although we saw in the horta a mother-figure protecting the physical existence of her young of either sex, we glimpse in *The Companion* a mother-figure in a special relationship to a human male. The *Enterprise's* shuttlecraft, transporting the ill Nancy Hedford to the starship for treatment, is diverted to Gamma Canaris N by a luminous cloud. Here the crew meet Zefram Cochrane, a pioneer in space exploration who is thought to have died 150 years earlier yet still looks young and healthy. Landing on this planet as an old man, he had been found by a sparkling light-being whom he calls *The Companion*, who rejuvenated him and now maintains him. Because he has become lonely and bored in this unchanging life, *The Companion* has brought him company in the form of the crew on the shuttlecraft, who are not allowed to leave.

Kirk reawakens Cochrane's interest in space and engages his cooperation in an attempt at escape. Since Cochrane is the only one who can communicate with *The Companion* as it surrounds him and interpenetrates with his body, he is to intercede for their release. When Spock ties the universal translator in to *The Companion's* wave length, Cochrane is shocked to discover that *The Companion's* voice is female. He is horrified that a feminine thing has entered his body. To the crew of the *Enterprise* his reaction seems antiquated and prejudiced, reminding us viewers that the formative period for Cochrane's ideas about sex would have been during the last half of the twentieth century.

The Companion has told the *Enterprise* crew that "the man," namely Cochrane, must survive at all costs. Kirk reads this as love and speculates that if he can only convince *The Companion* that Cochrane must leave the protection and monotony of the planet to survive, she will relinquish him for his own good. Nancy Hedford proves to be another disposable female as she weakens toward death from an illness which is fatal if untreated. Looking back over her life, Nancy laments her lack of a genuine love relationship. *The Companion,* by taking over the body of the dying Nancy, incidentally redeems her life's emptiness and opens a new channel of communication with Cochrane on the basis of equality. *The Compan-*

ion is willing to sacrifice eternal existence in order to be with Cochrane in a way which fulfills his psychic needs. She cannot leave her native planet and he is unwilling to leave her new form since he owes his very existence to her nurture. Together they will farm to meet their physical needs and perhaps even raise children, who would symbolize their ideal unity as a human couple.

Although Spock figures less centrally in this episode, he does, by adapting and employing the universal translator, provide the means for making *The Companion* aware of the needs of the others she is involved with. Even though *The Companion* will not let him touch her, Spock manages to find a channel of communication, as he did with the horta. What continues to be missing is a mother interacting fruitfully with her daughter. *The Companion*, after functioning as a mother, becomes a wife, an unusual progression to say the least.

The Illusionist Mother: *The Menagerie*

We have moved through a trio of destructive Mother figures to the physically protective horta and to *The Companion* who adapts herself to the psychic needs of Cochrane by assuming human form. In the inner plot of *The Menagerie*, extracted from the first *Star Trek* pilot, *The Cage*, we meet the Talosians, who further develop the idea of Mother. They compose a trio of old women, who like the horta, live underground. Although they can appear on the surface of their earth, Talus IV, they lack the physical strength to transform its inhospitable surface. They specialize in mental transformations—the endlessly variable world of illusion. The mental, symbolized by their large, pulsating heads, gives form to their physical world. Telepathically they can read the mind of anyone in a state of desire and then project an embodiment of what he or she wants. Where the horta could respond to the physical dimension of existence, and *The Companion* could adapt to psychic needs, the Talosians move even further in this direction and use the mental to reshape the physical.

As *The Companion* rejuvenated Cochrane and maintained his form, so the Talosians have restored Vina, a young woman injured in a spaceship crash on their planet. In this way the Talosians share nurturing motherhood with *The Companion*. Not knowing what humans look like, however, they did not do an aesthetically pleasing job. Although their powers of illusion compensate for any physical deformity or malfunction, Vina can never leave their planet and their illusory powers. Thanks to the Talosian power of illusion, however, she can take any form she desires. Thus, when the Talosians want her to mate with Pike, then captain of the *Enterprise,* and generate a race strong enough to colonize the surface of their planet, she appears to him as a Rigellian in distress, a seductive Terran woman, and finally an Orion belly dancer. She is the perfect *anima,* able to vary her appearance according to the whims of the male fantasy. Like the salt-sucking monster in *Man Trap*, she combines substantiality with the ability to materialize the forms desired by the opposite sex.

As the horta could, through the mediation of

Spock, be helpful to the miners, so the Talosians can aid the injured Pike given Spock's help in transporting him there, the chief issue in the framing plot of the two-part *Menagerie*. A re-illusioned Pike can enjoy the reillusioned Vina, even though both must remain in the underworld of Talos IV. Without the Talosian mothers, Vina would become ugly just as Mudd's women without the love crystals feel ugly. Through taking the appearance of the ideal feminine as it exists in the male psyche, Vina becomes beautiful, though she is perpetually dependent on the creative powers of illusion practiced by the Talosian mothers. Since the mothers create Vina's beauty, she is in effect their creation, their daughter, a daughter who is, however, incapable of emerging into independence from them. Although a form of the mother-daughter relationship emerges here, it remains rudimentary and mainly in service of male fantasy.

Although the Talosians save Vina, their motives at first are not purely benevolent. They wish to breed a subservient race to develop their planet for them. Hence, they try to capture the healthy Pike for the purpose of breeding with Vina. The younger Pike's capacity for self-assertion, to the point of preferring death to servitude, convinces the Talosians that they do not want to take humans captive. They also recognize that the imposition of their world on a whole healthy human would be an act of destruction.

The Matriarchal Mother: *Amok Time*

As Spock was the agent for Pike's transfer to Talos IV, so he is the means by which we visit

Vulcan and witness the *pon farr* rituals. Without him these worlds would be outside the range of the *Enterprise*. Whereas in *The Menagerie*, mother and daughter share dependence on illusion, in *Amok Time* they combine to form a common female presence which expresses itself through shared loyalty to traditional ritual. Although T'Pring has the choice of whether or not to challenge her childhood betrothal to Spock, she must follow the traditional forms over which T'Pau, the Vulvan matriarch, presides. Although there is no sexual or even physical contact between the sexes, women preside over the rules within which Spock must work out this seizure by unconscious and instinctual drives. Through following the prescribed rules, in particular the ritual combat with father-figure Kirk, Spock dramatizes a necessary step in integration. When he finds that Kirk is not dead, that his captain has been resurrected, so to speak, Spock can express genuine joy, one of those human emotions long suppressed within him. If the mating ritual symbolizes increased maturity for the male, the same ritual symbolizes for the female union with the matriarch, the mother-figure, in loyalty to tradition.

As we saw in relation to McCoy, the feminine is frequently associated with the conservative function of tradition. Associated with the body, she is conserver of the body politic as we see in other episodes as well. Natira in *For the World is Hollow and I Have Touched the Sky* is the priestess who receives the word of the Oracle and transmits it to the people. Similarly, in Spock's *Brain* the priestess can put on her head the *Teacher* and act on the basis of his instruction. She supplies the body, he the brain. His is the accumulation of past knowledge, hers is the transmission and application of it. In *That Which Survives,* it is once again a woman who perpetuates the values of her people even after death—hers and theirs.

In the world of the *Enterprise*, with its mission to bring the unknown into the light of consciousness, the identification of the feminine with the conservation of past knowledge and tradition is not sufficient. Change and growth, as Spock says in *Let That Be Your Last Battlefield*, are necessary to life; subservience to tradition only stultifies individuals and their worlds, as we can see again and again in episodes like *The Apple, A Taste of Armageddon, The Return of the Archons,* and *The Cloud-Miners,* among many others.

In several scripts, we have seen Spock in his special relationship to the alien, especially the alien as feminine, as destructive mother. Unlike Kirk, who never gets involved with older women (*Miri*), Spock has unique access to the older, negative feminine presence. He has access to that which would prove physically or emotionally fatal to others: he can enter the cosmic amoeba, he can communicate with the horta and the Talosians. He can penetrate the formerly forbidden innards of the *prima materia* even in its connection with the underworld.

The horta is also linked with the earth goddess Demeter, who out of grief for the abduction of her daughter Persephone by the god of the underworld, thwarts all productivity. It was through her that the Greeks explained winter:

spring came only when Persephone was allowed to return to her mother on the earth. The horta, however, can never appear on the face of the earth, either physically, because of her material nature, or psychically, since she lacks the speech that would allow her an independent relationship with the masculine world that exists there. She is both *prima materia*, the earth mother, and the daughter who shares her mother's substance and serves in the underworld of men.

Spock's capacity to bring to the light of consciousness feminine mysteries within the context of *Star Trek* scripts finds its echo in Spock's impact on the viewing public, especially the women. In the outside world, where *Star Trek* reaches its viewers, Spock's impact may well be even more potent. The following chapter will deal with him as a masculine projection from the feminine psyche, as an archetypal figure who can bring women into fuller access to their own minds and selves.

Our voyaging is only great circle sailing,
Direct your right eye inward, and you'll find
A thousand regions in your mind
Yet undiscovered. Travel then, and be
Expert in home-cosmography.

Thoreau

10 We Are All Spock

In examining the disposable female, we had a
first look at the working of psychosexual encounter in *Star Trek*, particularly in the many encounters between Kirk and beautiful young
women, who (one at a time) embodied his internal ideal of the feminine projected into the
outer world. Implicitly, these *anima*-figures allow
Kirk to relate to the unconscious feminine part
of his own psyche. Naturally enough for the hero
of the show, he proves to have good psychological balance. For example, he outwits several
anima-figures who would like to control him. In
episodes like *Catspaw* and *By Any Other Name*,
he consciously plays up to women for his own
purposes. He knows his emotions and keeps them

under control in a way that would be impossible if his internal feminine side were unintegrated, because in that case he would be uncontrallably attracted to and under the power of those figures.

This chapter is primarily concerned with the opposite psycho-sexual encounter—between women and their *animus* projections, another context in which Spock is the key character. Though Spock serves this function in a way quite different from that of Kirk, Jung once again is the source of the concepts which allow us to see what is going on behind the scenes in *Star Trek*.

Visually speaking, the essential polarities of gender are represented in the opposition between the circular and the straight we remarked in the starship *Enterprise* itself, or the vulva and the phallus prominent in so many of the world's religions. In Jung's conception of the human psyche, there is a comparable balance of opposition between the *anima* and the *animus*. As the *anima* is a psychological image of the essence of the feminine embedded in the male psyche, so the *animus* is the perfectly masculine projected out of the female psyche. According to the Jungian scheme, the masculine is represented by intellect in the north and sensation in the west, corresponding to the oriental notion of *yang*, and the feminine is the dark area containing the feelings in the south and the intuitions in the east, which corresponds to the *yin*.

Actual males and females are, of course, not perfect specimens of the masculine and the feminine; nonetheless, owing to socialization based on traditional definitions of sexual distinctions, most men are dominantly masculine, most women dominantly feminine. Even so, just as the *yin* area has within it a portion of the masculine *yang*, and the *yang* area a portion of the *yin*, so men and women have within themselves their contrasexual opposites, *anima* and *animus* respectively. Even though a man may not be perfectly masculine, nor a woman perfectly feminine, their projected opposites tend to conform to the gender archetypes.

Insofar as one rejects in oneself characteristics of the opposite sex, *animus* or *anima* remains relatively underdeveloped and undifferentiated. They remain unconscious and begin to dictate a person's behavior. For example, a man who has not integrated his *anima* seeks the satisfaction of his vanity, which, Jung suggests, women may easily fulfill at the beauty parlor. A woman who has not integrated her *animus* seeks the power found by men through their positions of importance in the world, though Jung does not make this last implication explicit.

When these sexually linked faculties remain unconscious and unintegrated, they feel foreign to us and are projected easily onto other persons of the opposite sex, particularly someone who assumes an unfamiliar air or a divine or semi-divine aura. The less in touch the individual is with his/her internal contrasexual opposite, the more god-like and overpowering the projected *anima* or *animus* will seem.

In *Space Seed*, we see a female crew member, Lieutenant McGivers, encountering a forceful leader from the past who has been in suspended animation. He is dark and authoritarian and embodies all those leadership qualities that characterize the memorable strong men of earth's history from Alexander the Great on. He asserts his will, takes her by gallant force, and offers her the chance to become the mother of a superrace. For a time she is so carried away that she is willing to betray Kirk and the *Enterprise* to help Khan attain his goal of universal domination. She reconsiders at the last moment and saves Kirk, who resumes command of the starship, but for her disobedience she is condemned to leave the *Enterprise*, either by courtmartial or by going with Khan to colonize a planet whose flora and fauna are sufficiently wild to tax even his physical prowess. Whereas Kirk feels no guilt after nearly betraying the *Enterprise* for Edith Keeler, McGivers makes no attempt to defend herself and opts to follow her *animus*-figure. She will go with Khan, who ends the episode with an echo of Lucifer's assertion that it is better to be free than to serve even the forces of light. She is condemned for attachment to her contrasexual opposite, precisely what Kirk enjoys with his many disposable women.

It is no surprise that the frequency with which Kirk encounters *anima*-women is out of balance with the frequency with which *Star Trek* women have comparable encounters with *animus*-men, since men have dominated Western culture for so many centuries. When a *Star Trek* female does meet an embodiment of her *animus*, the result is usually disastrous to her. One important exception occurs when a woman succeeds in mastering her own inclination to bow before the masterful *animus*.

Mastering the Animus: Who Mourns for Adonais?[1]

When the *Enterprise* is grabbed in space by a huge hand, its owner demands that Kirk beam down and then bow down to worship him. Apollo demonstrates the power to increase to gigantic size and to immobilize phasers. He convinces the landing party that he is indeed a survivor of the Greek gods, who suddenly appear to have been early space travellers who tired of Earth once their worshippers fell away. One member of the landing party is a woman, Lieutenant Carolyn Palamas, who is a specialist in archeology and ancient civilizations. Apollo is delighted by her beauty, which he enhances in both his and her own eyes by instantly reclothing her in flowing Greek robes. He wants the *Enterprise* crewmen to worship him in the manner of the shepherds of classical Greece, but most of all he wants Carolyn to become his Queen, a near-goddess and the mother of a new and majestic race. Carolyn's response is typical *animus* possession—she is flattered, delighted, and acquiescent. It is as if her wildest dreams were suddenly coming true. What more could one ask for? Kirk, of course, wants the ship to be freed to continue its mission rather than to tend sheep and gather laurel leaves in perpetual obeisance to Apollo. And Kirk is the instrument of awakening Carolyn's inner control

1. *Adonais* derives from a semitic root meaning *master,* thus implicitly extending the resonance of the episode beyond the specific cultural prototype found in the character of Apollo.

over herself, which in turn is crucial to liberty for
the whole ship. Kirk appeals to her in the name
of duty and loyalty to humankind. She is not a
Greek goddess but a human, and hence she has
no business marrying a creature of such a radically different nature.

The means Carolyn finds within herself to
reestablish self-mastery are important to note
because they are the masculine faculties of sensation and intellect that Apollo as *animus*-figure
wanted her to forget in becoming the perfect
woman to match his divine manhood. She begins
to think of Apollo not as a god but as a subject
for anthropological study whom she is observing
and analyzing. These masculine mental activities
distance her from her own internal feminine
faculties of feeling and intuition and thereby
distance her from Apollo. Once she rejects him,
Apollo's fury begins to weaken him and finally,
once the *Enterprise* has destroyed his temple with
phaser bombardment, the god just disappears.
Apollo, like Eden, is obsolete and his vanishing
reminds us that in psychological terms he was
above all an insubstantial projection of Carolyn's
unconscious and previously unintegrated *animus*.
She will be a more integrated person, more captain of herself from this experience on.

Spock as Archetype

In Jung's understanding of the human psyche,
the unconscious buried faculties and contrasexual
images can become integrated into the psyche
primarily through the intervention of an archetype, that is, an entity or figure who because partly

human and partly nonhuman can mediate between the conscious mind and the hidden unconscious. Number, by having both a qualitative and a quantitative dimension, is such an archetype, as is the hybrid, the half-human half-other figure. Obviously the world of *Star Trek* offers a rich archetypal figure in the person of Spock.

Spock as archetype is part of a long tradition of half-human half-alien beings which have peopled folklore and plagued moralists for centuries. Most of his predecessors, however, were half-human half-animal, with the result that, like the Greek satyrs or Pan, they were often condemned in Western culture as aggressive and diabolical, alien forces to be feared and rejected.

Spock's specialness or alienness is sometimes expressed in terms recalling his predecessors. He is identified with the god Pan by Apollo in *Who Mourns for Adonais?*; in *Shore Leave* he beams down on a waning energy circuit and hovers a moment elevated on a rock, a luminous ithyphallic deity; his pointed ears recall the Christian devil as McCoy delights in pointing out; once he briefly even sports a halo; in *The Paradise Syndrome* he can do what had been anticipated only from the gods. However, unlike his avatars in the past, associated as they were with the underworld, the bestial, blood, suffering, violent sexuality, Spock is not half-human half-animal but half-human half-Vulcan. His specialness comes from association with a superior world of the mind.

As we saw in *Amok Time* Spock symbolically transforms a form of sexuality usually considered typical of the female animal—heat—so that it makes contact with the conscious mind.

The sexual is not eliminated but elevated beyond both physical mechanics and social preconceptions to its significance for the individual conscious mind. Thus we have a figure which can genuinely function for women as an archetype, as a mirror within and a door to further consciousness. Spock's masculinity is enhanced by his mental powers. Not only are they considered masculine in themselves, but they are of sufficient strength to control a superior male body. Controlled, this masculinity can be put at the service of individual men and women such as those Spock works with on the *Enterprise* or such as we are. Here the magic power is not limited to one human organ or tradition and hence it maintains its universality.

The logic with which Spock controls his emotions contributes directly to his sex appeal to female viewers. Pure union of soul is not compromised by idiosyncratic like or dislike of the shape of somebody's body or the color of skin (or carapace in the case of the horta). Union between the sexes can regain a lost innocence when a sharing of minds precedes or even substitutes for a union of bodies, as we see in Spock's relationship with the Romulan captain in *The Enterprise Incident*. The reign of logic guarantees the purity of emotions in Spock as stimulus to fruitful female fantasy.

Unlike the *animus*-figures which Emma Jung encountered in women's dreams, Spock is not an authority figure. He improves upon the traditions passed on as holy on some planets—or "repairs" them as he did in *The Paradise Syndrome*—but he does not represent authority.

Whereas previous divinities were concerned with imparting the Word embodied in a fixed tradition, his semidivine overtones consist in his being able to modify past bodies of knowledge and adapt them to an unprecedented present situation. No woman can relate to him as Natira in *For the World Is Hollow and I Have Touched the Sky* relates to the Oracle. She is the body which transmits the message of its computerized mind to the people. Although the Oracle represents mind, it is fixed in a social form that demands undue reverence for what proves to be fallible guidance.

Star Trek consistently shows up the flaws in giving undue reverence to the past. In *A Piece of the Action,* we visit a society which accidentally retained from an earlier Federation visit a history book describing the gangland activities in Chicago in the 1930s. This text was taken as revealed scripture coming from the heavens, and the "bosses" proceeded to shape a whole way of life —and death—in imitation of what appeared to be ideal.

Patterns of Force places the naive obeisance to history in yet another perspective. Here Star Fleet historian John Gill attempts to isolate and recreate on Ekos just one apparently desirable aspect of the past—the efficient organization of Nazi Germany. Once again, we see that absolute authority leads to unlimited destructiveness.

Spock could never fall into such a trap. He shows us how survival in the fullest sense depends on freeing oneself from a past one learns from and therefore can build upon. In *Star Trek* we see that one is condemned to repeat what one has not *understood*.

Spock is a crucial figure, as we have seen, in modifying structures from the past which have become destructive through inappropriate repetition. He represents an important innovation on the traditional authority figure, which is particularly relevant to women and their relationship to the *animus*.

According to Emma and Carl Jung, the *animus* in women has traditionally been projected onto figures who, invested with authority from the past, demand submission. Since Western society has surrounded women with a great many such figures—priests, ministers, teachers, doctors, dentists, or policemen, for example—the *animus* as projected in dreams was similarly diffuse and fragmentary. In addition when such authority figures appeared in dreams as *animus* projections they retained an aura appropriate to their social station. Thus, for the individual woman, the *animus* often seems external to her, overpowering and disparate, hence dangerous and difficult to relate to. This situation is nicely dramatized in *The Return of the Archons* where any male villager can address a dignitary's daughter, a grown woman, as if she were a child. He asks if her "daddy" could not lodge the *Enterprise* landing party. The same woman later falls victim to implied rape during the yearly "carnival" of organized violence. The male in the mind of a woman becomes synonymous with an authority too august to be understood or integrated into herself.

Spock, on the other hand, offers women a figure who is both archetypically male and because of his Vulcan powers able to move beyond forms of authority traditionally identified with men. He reaches out to individual women in a way that is unprecedented in television viewing history.

Spock and His Fans

Spock's special status on the *Enterprise* as its resident alien has special consequences for his fans. His archetypal resonance emerges not so much in relation to the few female characters who get close to him but rather in his impact on female viewers of the series. Although all the actors in the series have their fan clubs, the Leonard Nimoy Fan Club, one of the first and largest, is 95 percent female. The primary activity is writing to fellow fans about the activities of Nimoy and others associated with *Star Trek*. There is also considerable emphasis on charitable activities, in part following Leonard Nimoy's own example. Gossip and volunteer work have long been thought appropriate activities for women, but such clubs have given rise to an activity new on such a scale for women—writing. If female characters on the show want to "have" Spock in the usual heterosexual way, many among his female fans have turned to writing to "have" him imaginatively. As Gene Roddenberry's creation of the characters relates parts of himself to each other in the form of Kirk and Spock, so I see these women trying to relate to a Spock within themselves and through his mediation to their own *animus*-selves.

Although within the world of *Star Trek* our Vulcan friend is the model of emotional control, many fan scripts turn on very explicit emotional or sexual encounters with female characters who break through his control. Gene Roddenberry has theorized that women want to penetrate his rationality so that they can relate to him emotionally, so that they can be *the* one to awaken the *real* Spock. Such is a traditionally womanly response, though it does not take into account the composite nature of the Leonard Nimoy Fan Club, which seems to bring together traditionally oriented women, who are concerned with the needs and affairs of others, and also the liberated women who can write sexually sophisticated *Star Trek* scripts. The authors of *Star Trek Lives!*[2] go further by speculating that as women become more liberated, they are drawn to the idea of a no-strings-attached affair of the sort a Spock implicitly promises.

A sexual encounter of this sort, as described in recent years by such writers as Kate Millett and Erica Jong, is an anonymous affair which reunites the sex act with a kind of moral purity. By removing sex from the complexities of personal taste, which is often based on attraction inspired by *animus*- or *anima*-projection (or both), and by cutting sex off from the complications of continuing relationships like marriage, the no-strings-attached affair seems ideal. It is, of course, itself a fantasy and hence, in Erica Jong's words, "rarer than a unicorn."[3] Now, thanks to Gene Rodden-

2. Jacqueline Lichtenberg, Sondra Marshak, Joan Winston, *Star Trek Lives!* (New York: Bantam Books, 1975), p. 223.
3. Erica Jong, *Fear of Flying* (New York: Signet, 1973), p. 14.

berry and Leonard Nimoy, the unicorn has been domesticated and is, if not quite in everyone's lap, at least in nearly everyone's living room. Spock, as a male figure who is as rare as a unicorn, is easily woven into the tapestries of women's dreams. He implicitly promises the perfect relationship. Through personal integrity he is free of intrigue and ulterior motive, and even in the heat of *pon farr* he proves incapable of the manipulative control that could turn a sexual encounter into a power play.

As Spock embodies emotional control, so he acts without need to seize power for himself. Once he has stimulated his fans' emotional fantasies, however, they can write potential television scripts with *women* in command of starships, often with Spock continuing as first officer. Since sexual fantasies and resulting scripts are images dramatizing psychic forces, the idea of a female starship captain expresses the ideal goal of being female *and* the kind of whole human being Captain Kirk represents, the ideal of being, in other words, captain of oneself as *woman*.

The welcome Spock receives from women who gravitate toward him as to a magnetic pole indicates the need for such a being. If scripts are written in which the essence of him seems to be located in the phallus, I do not really think that it is the penis they are after any more than in *Spock's Brain* it was his physical organ which could ultimately solve the problems of the Morgs and the Eymorgs. In both cases, it is Spock as self, as he can be realized in one's own being; this is the challenge with which Kirk left Kara, the brain-thief. A Spock lost in an unconscious wallow of emotion, as was forced on him in *Plato's Step-children,* will die as surely as a Spock lost in the unconsciousness of being without a brain. He could never become the mindless follower of a Holy Program.

Nor, happily, could he become the enforcer of such a program. A brief look at *The Empath* will provide an interesting comparison with *Spock's Brain.* In the latter a population of women have let their own minds atrophy through lack of use; therefore, they depend on the *Teacher*, which transmits to them the content of past knowledge, and on stolen brains to provide intellectual motive power for the community. In *The Empath* we see men who impose intellectually conceived moral imperatives on a mute female empath. They, devoid of human feelings themselves, test the "purity" of her feelings by demanding that she become a willing human sacrifice. These men feed on her feeling as the Eymorgs feed on Spock's brain. The Vian men who act entirely on preconceived ideas are as destructive as the women who have no ideas. Both embody imbalances which can only consume others. Spock is mediator between the two extremes. He directs the restoration of his brain to his own body, which in the long run obliges the women to cultivate their own intellectual powers. Then, along with Kirk, he convinces the Vians that Gem's willingness to sacrifice herself for McCoy need not be lived out in gory detail. Spock cannot be contained in one pole or the other. Spock lives.

Spock as independent fiction free to travel in everyone's mind, as a being who is known yet who does not exist, is available to everyone and can meet any of us where we are. He can be written into orgiastic scripts or any other kind of script. If some women *really* want to marry him, others may find that to their (pleasant) surprise they have. An acquaintance of ours wanted to go to the university after marriage but learned that her husband felt such activity was inappropriate for a young wife and mother. After seeing and admiring Spock, however, he tried to incorporate Spock's characteristics into his own life. The husband soon realized that there is no logical reason why women should not study; his wife is now in college. The Spock born in the imagination of Gene Roddenberry and brought alive by Leonard Nimoy continues to evolve in the imagination of many—a part of us all and property of none.

The Evolution of Spock

The evolution of Spock becomes relevant here. It is great good luck when the need to project and relate to a given psychic content corresponds with the opportunity to do so. The emergence of the character Spock is an example of such luck combined with human intelligence and integrity. In Gene Roddenberry's original pilot *The Cage*, Number One is the second in command. She is coolly logical as well as dark, mysterious, nameless—at least as long as she existed—and female. Spock in the pilot was the science officer, the alien, a bit eager, a bit wet behind the latex ears. Roddenberry's sensitivity to the needs and capacities of women was not appreciated by network officials, who told him that the highly placed woman had to go. Although she hardly played a dominant role in *The Cage,* she was considered too bossy. Spock also fell under attack: no one would accept an alien in family viewing time, the network said. Roddenberry thought he could keep one of the two characters and decided to put the characteristics of Number One into Spock and then marry Number One himself. That is, as Roddenberry enjoys remarking, he married actress Majel Barrett who played the part of Number One, something he could not have done with Leonard Nimoy, who plays Spock!

Chance enhanced Roddenberry's good intentions: Spock is, I think, more important for women than Number One could ever have been. As a woman, not an alien, the most a successful Number One could have provided would have been a good example, a model of the highly placed and competent woman. She might have had the kind of appeal for women that Kirk does for men as an idealized model of success, which though certainly palpable, is nothing new. In spite of the existence of models, the problem always remains: how to realize a comparable success.

Once Gene Roddenberry had succeeded in preserving Spock as a character, another man's contribution became important to building and maintaining the archetypal resonance of the figure. Leonard Nimoy was always the actor Roddenberry had in mind for Spock. Although Nimoy has always emphasized his professionalism as an actor, others—from Gene Roddenberry to the authors of *Star Trek Lives!*—have highlighted his integrity. Both characteristics seem relevant.

The need for good acting is obvious; we have in *I Am Not Spock*[4] a very nice description of Leonard Nimoy's sense of himself as an actor and of what was involved in the creation of Spock. Spock's depth of character developed as Nimoy listened to the feedback from Spock's impact. He incorporated these insights into his interpretation of the character in various episodes. Professionalism needed integrity even at the beginning; Nimoy had to defend Spock so that he would in no script betray himself, compromise his character, lose his identity. Nimoy's perception of Spock's special relationship to emotion and his mother Amanda led to his building the crucial scene in *The Naked Time*. He felt the episode to be a turning point; I feel it is also a metaphor for the way Spock could borrow Nimoy the actor to make himself known to us.

Once Spock was established, however, Nimoy faced different challenges. He saw that Spock could easily become a pop culture hero, something he had not bargained for. Having let Spock borrow him, he could have insisted that Spock keep him; he could have accepted the invitation to become a kind of guru. He has been asked to heal with his Vulcan powers, to contact extraterrestrials, and a lesser person might have agreed to do so for the right price.

Spock does have obvious similarities to the non-Western gurus who have flourished in recent years in the United States and Europe. They have in common at least a shared foreignness and

4. Leonard Nimoy, *I Am Not Spock* (Millbrae, California: Celestial Arts, 1975).

"exotic" mental powers. Common attributes also include training in concentration, a vegetarian diet, knowledge of arcane secrets (including occult physiologies like acupuncture charts), direct mental knowledge of another, mental control of the emotions and pain. Gurus, however, are people; Spock is not. Gurus are examples, models to be emulated. Had Nimoy given his offstage self over to public exploitation of Spock, the combination could have had the aura of medicine-show charlatanism. If the real guru lies in our inner Spocks which we project outward upon actual people, it is easier to know this part of ourselves through a fictional character than through another person to whom the characteristics seem to belong. Science fiction lets us move into the world of the imagination freed from the baggage of everyday realities, and Spock can become a mirror of ourselves.

Leonard Nimoy could have greatly reduced Spock's resonance, perhaps even have destroyed it, had he encouraged the identity of himself with Spock that so many fans would have gladly applauded. To lock Spock into one body is to encourage one to see him as less than he is: archetypal figure available to all our imaginations.

Although there are Spock fans at conventions who have Spock ears applied and assume Vulcan names, they may not be simply impersonating Spock but rather acting out what they feel in themselves to be Vulcan. Spock is not a model which presents us with one, albeit exemplary, way of doing things; he serves instead as a window opening on possibilities which we then must apply in our own lives. As it is Kirk who translates

Spock's superior knowledge and intellect into action, so it is every individual Spock fan who must do the same in his own life. We are not given a blueprint to copy but a part of ourselves which we must incorporate into our lives as best we can. Number One was a woman, 51 percent of us are women; Spock is an alien, part of *all* of us is alien. Number One might have been a model for female success, but Spock is a challenge, especially for women. The challenge is how to realize oneself more fully.

Towards a Western Yoga

Since Leonard Nimoy has preserved the integrity of Spock, he can communicate to us religious implications that go far beyond the standard guru trip. Instead of importing religious traditions or practices from the East, Spock points the way to potentially important developments that can build on our own cultural tradition. In India, for example, there exist elaborate systems such as those found in Tantric yoga which consider the genitals the seat of vital force which can rise through several centers to terminate and find fruition in the mind. Years ago, however, Jung pointed out that in the West the locus of this energy was in the head, not the gonads. He hoped that eventually there would evolve in the West a yoga which would reverse Tantric conceptions. The latter leads one upward and out, using sexual intercourse as a means to reaching mental communion and stability. The new yoga should lead one inward and down, where Spock in fact takes us. The word *yoga* means "to link" and we feel that Spock has a mental network connecting his inner and outer selves. Spock responds to the mating urge but transforms it into a ritual signifying not its physical mechanics but its psychic significance. Similarly, when he must repair a mechanical computer program meant to contain the Holy Program of some society, he moves beyond the mechanics which would bind people in a fixed social body and changes the program of the past to respond to a present in a way which could lead to a future. Through his Vulcan mind, expressed in his whole way of being, he provides the means to be lucid in sexual ecstasy or social intercourse. Whereas previous deities have tended to trap women in a physical body or in social roles, Spock offers them a mind through which they might emerge into their own.

Spock's mental powers and their function of consciousness further make him important in just those ways in which he differs from earlier half-alien hybrids. To a woman influenced or formed by traditional ideas of femininity, the phallus as sexual symbol can only invite another descent into the unconscious with which she is already identified. As long as the feminine continues to be defined in terms of the emotional and intuitive, she can only find in the phallus a symbol for sexual union as unconsciously emotional or "romantic" experience. We find encouragement for this identification in every cliché about love. As we saw in relation to McCoy, the romantic has been traditionally defined as emotional: one should be swept off one's feet, carried away. One is supposed to meet one's mate in exotic medieval dress or bunny costume, not in work clothes. The Great Relationship, like Eden, is as all embracing and unconditional as the Oracle's Instrument of Obedience in *For the World Is Hollow and I Have Touched the Sky,* which admits no collective bargaining.

What I wish to speculate on here is a Spock made accessible to the feminine not by changing Spock but by changing the notion of what women can and perhaps ought to become. Incorporating the *animus* is not to be done by excising Vulcan masculinity, but by enlarging the woman to be able to incorporate it into her own life. Just as Erica Jong's novel expresses dissatisfaction with intercourse "zippered up" in everyday sex and emotions, so a Spock succumbing to these would compromise his appeal.

Just as the man whose wife wanted to study learned through Spock to deal with the validity of her desire, so in larger terms Spock can lead one to an appreciation of desire, of thrust, in either sex. A traditionally feminine fear of flying is not going to be overcome by taking Spock out of the air; flight is essential to the *Enterprise.* The challenge is for women themselves to emerge into flight.

Religious Implications

On a more philosophical level, Spock as an archetypal figure offers a new avenue to the unknown, a new way of dealing with the unconscious. The old ways of encountering the unknown have been colored by patriarchal religion transmitted by men concerned with their *anima.* To see this we have only to look at what the word *religion* has come to mean. The church fathers set its interpretation when they claimed it derived from the Latin word *religo, -are,* which means *to bind.* McCoy continues the same line each time he lectures Spock on the value of a love defined unconsciously, as if Spock could not love because of his omnipresent consciousness. Such a concept of emotional love has been a catalyst for the men who have created what we know as Western civilization. Just as we saw Kirk in *Shore Leave* finding rest and recreation in his contact with Ruth, the materialization of his dreams of woman, so men throughout the history of the West have found their creative energies regenerated by the Muse, the *anima*-woman, whose femininity complements those characteristics they identify themselves with. By formulating the unknown in terms of what men consider to be their opposite, the feminine values of emotion and intuition as love, men have so structured the universe that it favors the renewal of their creative energies. Love as the supreme expression of the Ultimate can at the same time reinforce masculine identity and regenerate it through the kind of energy that can only flow from creative tension between polarities. Since, however, opposition is spontaneously expressed in terms of sexual differences, women tend to be identified with the *anima* ideal. Insofar as a woman must grasp her identity in terms of men's ideals, it is difficult for her to imagine her own ideals, that is, what she would find fulfilling for herself. We are now beginning to realize how women have been left in the lurch. With the universe defined in terms suitable to male fantasy, there was little room for female fantasies to populate the heavens. Lacking this pole of opposition, there was little room for creative sparks to flash between women and their own unknown inner spaces. They did not have the images through which to engage in their own enterprise of unification of opposites.

Religo, -are is not the only possible root and direction for *religion*. As Jung points out there is also *relego, -ere*,[5] which implies paying close attention to the numinous, the unconscious, especially to that which arises from the unconscious as particularly imposing, Apollo for example. If a man needs to practice love as a means to incorporate his *anima,* a woman needs to pay close attention to projected male figures in order to incorporate her *animus*.

The world of the *Enterprise* presents a new possibility for women. Even though there are no highly placed women on the crew, Spock opens more possibilities than would a female second officer. By communicating with the rejected feminine, Spock opens the way for a new appreciation of the Old Woman or the Evil Woman, the Devil in the Dark. By inspiring so many women to write scripts for him, Spock becomes a model for imaginative encounter with the buried self and encourages the process of critical imagining that can lead to psychic integrity. Because he is suited to our culture and because he is a product of it, Spock can speak to women more effectively than hybrids from the past such as Pan. The man within the woman, like the woman within the man,

5. Jung, 11:596.

slumbers in the head of contemporary humans, waiting for a Spock to help them emerge. Through such consciousness the human enterprise becomes the quasi-religious activity of relating opposites to each other, of becoming human beings able to function in the world of the present *and* the future.

The power of the world works in circles
and every thing tries to be round.

Black Elk

11 The Archetypal as Enterprise

The union of opposites has a long history in the
West and was at one time in our history considered a genuinely spiritual activity, although it
fell well outside the parameters of the official
church hierarchy. Contrary to some popular
opinions, medieval alchemy was not abortive
chemistry. Simple manipulation of materials
was left to the "puffers," inferior persons who
lacked the moral stature to pursue the true goal
of alchemy but who could do rudimentary experiments. The true goal of alchemy was the
union of opposites, by means of which man could
appear as a god-like microcosm, the divine androgyne, the one in whom all is unified. Like
flying, this goal was considered by many to be
unnatural, a *res contra naturam*. Like flying, al-

chemy was an art and a science, the result of
concentrated effort. Although cast in the termi-
nology of prechemistry, the goal was spiritual.
The processes by which the alchemists hoped to
transmute everyday metals into gold or the
sought-after philosopher's stone merely symbolized those processes by which they sought
spiritual wholeness. These constituted the *Mag-
num Opus,* the Great Work, the Enterprise; they
take place in the *athanor,* the vessel to which heat
is applied, "the fire-ship," from which the *lapis,*
the philosopher's stone, the golden nugget, will
emerge. This sought-for gold became synonymous with the golden temple, the light at the
center of a *mandala,* the fullness of human consciousness.

> By the philosophers I am named Mercurius; my
> spouse is the [philosophic] gold; I am the old
> dragon found everywhere on the globe of earth,
> father and mother, young and old, very strong
> and very weak, death and resurrection, visible and
> invisible, hard and soft; I descend into the earth
> and ascend to the heavens, I am the highest and
> the lowest, the lightest and the heaviest; often the
> order of nature is reversed in me, as regards color,
> number, weight and measure; I contain the light
> of nature; I am dark and light; I come forth from
> heaven and earth; I am known and yet do not
> exist at all; by virtue of the sun's rays all colors
> shine in me, and all metals. I am the carbuncle of
> the sun, the most noble purified earth, through
> which you may change copper, iron, tin, and lead
> into gold.[1]

Thus the duality of the alchemical Mercury, another image for the multiple dualities that we

1. Jung, 13:218.

have seen structuring the world of *Star Trek,* is described.

Unconscious Union of Opposites: *The Apple*

As the idea of the union of opposites has had a long history in the West, so have various images for the primal substance/energy of the universe, both as the preexistent matrix of being and as a final goal of individual evolution. In *The Apple* we see the creature Vaal, who is neither male nor female, and who maintains a society characterized by undifferentiated bliss. There is no aging, no death, no sexual awareness, no assaults on the life of another. Vaal becomes a figure for the *uroboros,* or cosmic dragon, who is self-begetting and self-consuming, the original serpent who spends eternity eating its tail—a *mandala* perhaps, though lacking a center.

The Apple begins with Kirk, Spock, McCoy and other crewmen beaming down to explore a mysterious planet. On finding it very much like Earth, they linger to take soil samples in spite of the death of one crewman. They discover a tribe of humanoids who are apparently the residents of this paradise; McCoy ascertains that they show no traces of deterioration or illness. They are in apparently perfect harmony with their environment and with themselves. They live in undifferentiated bliss. Their only duty is the regular and ritual feeding of Vaal.

Vaal presents itself to us as a dragon head opening out from the earth. Its force field controls the entire environment and now locks the

Enterprise in its gravitational pull. In its power are all the forces of heaven and earth; it provides nourishment and regulates the environment so that there is neither birth nor death; it counters aggression with electrical storms. Little by little the crew of the *Enterprise* watch its ritual feeding and discover that its grasp on the starship is weaker just before it eats. True to their notion of a balanced universe in which there are no infinite beings, they attack it with the *Enterprise's* phasers after having blocked its nourishment. Thus the dragon is spilt in two and destroyed with the fiery sword of the phaser beam and the world of unselfconscious *being* is shattered by the opposing forces characteristic of the world of *becoming*.

Before returning to the *Enterprise*, Kirk addresses the natives on the joys of sexual differentiation and the rewards of meeting the challenges posed by work. Theirs is no longer a self-contained world which consumes and begets itself, imaged perfectly by the tribe going down into the mouth of the dragon with their offerings. This uroboric self-containment, a hieroglyph for eternity, has encountered change. The cosmic egg has been split and from it individuals emerge. Kirk tries to communicate to them the joy of individual becoming in a world subject to opposites like female-male, life-death, young-old, good-bad.

Dynamic Equilibrium

Even when such episodes take us into a situation reminiscent of the human past, the perspective is still new. The medium which transmits these adventures is from the twentieth century. The television set, like the *Enterprise,* is a product of this century's imagination. Each hour-long episode is self-contained and appears in a series of television programs. Similarly, each adventure of the *Enterprise* is a unit which usually opens and closes on the bridge. Thus each hour can present us with not only a different subject but even a different perspective on a similar subject.

In the past, mythological expressions of the human psyche were fixed in the framework of a given society at a given time. Certain myths and archetypes were central to a given culture's identity and if they changed at all it was only gradually over the space of several generations. Such images were considered sacred Scripture in specific times and places. The world of *Star Trek,* on the other hand, ranges across infinitely varied possibilities, past, present, and future. Each episode's particular perspective is self-contained and stands in no essential sequential relationship to any other. Energies once tied to the symbols preferred by the perspective of a single society have been freed to locate themselves throughout inner as well as outer space. Thus, in a series of episodes, we can range through different times and spaces and encounter, on various other planets, archetypes previously thought by some human beings somewhere to reveal the essence of the universe. *Star Trek,* instead of elaborating a single worldview, is a work in progress, the enterprise of individuation or soul-making. The *Enterprise* even as an archetypal union of opposites is not a metaphor for universality; through it we continue to encounter new worlds, some more, some less advanced. In *The Return of the Archons*, the *Enterprise* might well be deified for freeing the world of Landru from slavery to a Holy Program, but in *Errand of Mercy* it must bow to the superiority of the Organians, who no longer need conflict and opposition as a means to evolution. Multiple perspectives open before us and invite us to undertake our own enterprise; scripts have replaced scripture.

In Jung's terms *Star Trek* presents us with the process of psychic evolution through which the conscious and the unconscious come together. In Claude Lévi-Strauss' terms, it invites us to take part in the making of living myth.

> And since the purpose of myth is to provide a logical model capable of overcoming a contradiction . . . a theoretically infinite number of slates [episodes] will be generated, each one slightly different from the others. Thus myth grows . . . until the intellectual impulse which has produced it is exhausted. Its *growth* is a continuous process, whereas its *structure* remains. . . . It closely corresponds, in the realm of the spoken word, to a crystal in the realm of physical matter.[2]

Although some fans may be disappointed that as this book goes to press, *Star Trek* will be continued as a television series rather than as a movie, its inner logic *is* episodic. Its world cannot be contained in one spectacular production; *Star Trek* does live.

Star Trek television scripts present a succession of archetypal figures which invite a limited

2. Claude Lévi-Strauss, *Structural Anthropology* (New York: Basic Books, Inc., 1963), p. 229.

number of responses. Their overwhelming or "numinous" character frequently invites the crew (and perhaps the viewers as well) to worship them or else flee them as devils. A third option, less socially acceptable, is to identify with them. All three of these possibilities place the *Enterprise* in jeopardy, since each in its own way would involve abandoning one term of the polarity crucial to the enterprise of unifying oppositions. If the crew were to worship one god-like figure such as Apollo or one ideal place such as Eden, their human consciousness would be denied and free movement abandoned. If they were to flee it, the unknown would be removed from the equation; if they were to identify with it, fusion would obliterate the terms of the contrast. The dramatic situation of *Who Mourns for Adonais?* turns on the danger posed by the first option—worship. *The Corbomite Manoeuver* turns on overcoming the desire to flee an apparent monster. *This Side of Paradise* is resolved by refusing to identify with a state of apparent perpetual bliss which would annihilate the personality as we know it. The fourth option in dealing with a given cultural archetype is, in fact, the only one that permits the continuation of the *Enterprise*. The terms of the polarities of conscious/unconscious or known/unknown must be dynamically maintained and brought into constantly new relationship to each other. All of the human capacities and functions are strained but ultimately strengthened as each episode ends with a return to the starship and usually to the bridge. As the chosen ones beam aboard on rays of light, the magic circle draws together again and the journey continues; the show must go on. A similar bridge of light gave access to the alchemical citadel, surrounding at its center the precious gold.

Union of Opposites in Consciousness: *Is There In Truth No Beauty?*

The precious gold of pure consciousness, however, can blind with its light just as surely as the pure unconsciousness imposed by Vaal kept his people in undifferentiated darkness. In this episode the key personage is Kollos, an ambassador from Medusa, whose bodiless presence is so powerfully blinding that mere humans go mad at the sight of him. The Medusans are pure light-and-enegry consciousness. The ambassador, housed in a special box more to protect others than himself, is beamed aboard with his "interpreter," the beautiful Miranda Jones. Though Spock is, as Kirk says, someone nothing gets to, even he must wear protective goggles at the point of meeting, that is, interpenetrating thoughts with the Ambassador.

Although Miranda is the ambassador's official guide, she reveals immediately a certain jealousy at Spock's capacity to greet the Medusan with apparently mutual comprehension. This attitude resurfaces at a formal dinner for her, where we learn that she is an empath who has been trained on Vulcan for her position on the Medusan planet and that her respect for Vulcan mental powers borders on envy. Whereas Spock speaks on the need for discipline to block out the bedlam of others' minds and emotions, she expresses the need to block out her own.

Larry, a human who loves her, is jealous of her preference for the Medusan ambassador. In his rage he attempts to kill Kollos but in the process of seeing him emerging from his box, goes mad. In his madness he dies, after he has taken over the engineering section and sent the *Enterprise* beyond the edge of the galaxy, where it can no longer locate coordinates to guide its movement. The ship itself is subjected to the starship equivalent of madness. Since Medusans have mastered intergalactic travel, Kollos could bring them back if they could find an intermediary. Spock, by means of the mind-meld, can let the Ambassador into his body and combine the latter's knowledge of intergalactic travel with his own knowledge of the *Enterprise*. Miranda in her jealousy forbids access to Kollos until the Ambassador himself is consulted and insists that Spock perform the meld to save the ship.

The Ambassador is brought to the bridge and, behind a screen, Spock unites with him. The ship's reentry into the galaxy is successful, but as the Ambassador is about to return to his box, we see that Spock, under the implied influence of Miranda, has forgotten his goggles. Without this added protection he too goes mad, and, totally turned in on himself, is taken to sick bay. At this point only Miranda can save him by means of the techniques learned on Vulcan; she is no longer wearing the sensor-dress, which has compensated for her physical blindness. In Kirk's words she is totally in the dark. In the depths of her darkness we see her finally turn to Spock and do the mild-meld for both their sakes. We learn that this is the first time she has performed such interpenetration, which has the effect of preparing her for uniting with the Medusan ambassador who has long since been freed from dependence on the physical.

The final scene is in the transporter room, where the episode began; we see Spock wishing her well and praising the philosophy of the IDIC pendant he is wearing: infinite diversity in infinite combinations. She for her part has known the joy of mind sharing and seems genuinely happy for the first time.

Throughout the episode the conflicts and dangers reiterate in dramatic terms the basic implications of *Star Trek* we have been probing all along. The tension between the known and the unknown is constant, reaching only temporary resolution at the end of this—and most other—episodes. The dangers are great also, because the being who goes too far or too quickly over to the unknown risks madness—like Larry, whose mind cannot cope with the Medusan's and hence goes insane, or like the *Enterprise,* which is thrown beyond our galaxy and risks being eternally lost to this world. Spock himself, despite his enormous powers of mind, can find himself overwhelmed by interpenetration with Kollos unless his goggles shield him from the full impact of the disembodied and unknown. The known can advance into the unknown and incorporate it only a bit at a time. Bringing to consciousness is an on-going and never-ending process which depends on keeping a reasonable balance between the opposites. When certain beings introduce too much alienness too quickly, like Charlie X in the episode which bears his name or the starship-devouring negative Mother figures out near the edge of the galaxy, they must be destroyed or returned to their own kind if the known world and its people are to survive.

Miranda Jones, through this episode, symbolizes the necessary balance. Miranda began by showing jealousy over Spock's Vulcan mental powers and wanting to keep Kollos all to herself. In this way she seems like a traditional female, wanting to mate with the masculine figure she idealizes. Kollos, however, is not just ordinarily masculine; his consciousness is so pure that it does not need a body to house it. Also, Miranda has prepared for union with him by several years of Vulcan mind training, which we have seen as symbol for all that is masculine. Hence her successful interpenetration, first with Spock, then with the Ambassador, transforms her own inner nature. By mastering her own inner masculine faculties and then sharing totally with a purely masculine being, she has achieved the ultimate union of gender opposites within herself. She emerges with the beatific smile of one who has achieved androgynous integration and need no longer feel jealousy over anything.

Miranda's beatific smile indicates that she has attained a new state of being, but all we can know is the process which led to it. The success of such a process is in fact determined by the degree of alienness a person can relate to at any one time. Any earlier interpenetration with Kollos might have left Miranda mad. Since survival is essential to growth, a person must reject what is destructively foreign, what is alien beyond the possibility of integration. Charlie X must be returned to his own world despite the crew's desire to socialize him enough to remain among humans. Similarly the cosmic amoeba in *The Immunity Syndrome* must be destroyed.

Nonetheless, the stuff of drama is individuals confronting opposites and moving in the direction of their integration. The concern is always with how characters move toward resolving their problems. To help visualize such movement, we can use a three-dimensional cube in order to visualize the interaction of the main polarities of *Star Trek*. By introducing an object, a cube, however, I am in the paradoxical situation of using an enclosed and static thing to diagram an open and continuing process. Nonetheless, the complexity of certain interrelationships can be better understood in three-dimensional terms.

A Space Cube

We have seen certain creative polarities within the *Enterprise*: the matter/antimatter engines; the circular and the straight shapes; the masculine and the feminine faculties as ways of approaching human experience. In addition, three sets of oppositions turn out to structure the episodes which unfold within and without the *Enterprise*: the polarities of morality, age, and gender. The following cube diagram will show the ways in which these three crucial polarities can be related to each other as interconnecting axes.

The poles of the age axis are represented as < for younger, > for older, those of the morality axis as + for good and − for evil; those of the gender axis by ♂ for male and ♀ for female. The single corner facing us here is the center from which virtually all action proceeds: the crew of the *Enterprise* are predominantly male, young, and good.

The function of the cube is not to circumscribe movement in a fixed structure, but to indicate the varieties of combinations which are possible. The drama of each episode occurs along linear axes, which can be represented as the edges of the cube, which are themselves defined and limited by the poles or apexes of the cube. The ideal characteristics represented by the poles may, of course, be beyond human capacities for knowing. Pure consciousness, the Medusan ambassador, like pure unconsciousness, is unknowable. The ideal poles are nonetheless hypotheses necessary for defining the axes along which the drama unfolds.

Any given episode can be positioned on the cube in a way which reveals its essential tensions and resolutions. Since many episodes involve either two or three of these axes, such a cube can help to visualize the interrelations between the significant factors. *Balance of Terror* presents us with the simplest of oppositions in terms of the Romulan commander as the older man and Kirk as the younger man.

The essential drama takes place along the single axis Romulan commander $(> + \male)$ versus Kirk $(< + \male)$. Although the first appearance of the Romulan commander suggests that the Romulans as enemies are paragons of evil comparable to the Klingons, we come to see the Commander as a worthy enemy and potential friend caught in a tightly defined militaristic system. The past history of the planet Vulcan, torn by violence, resurfaces in the Romulan way of life—and death. The Romulan commander, bound by loyalty to the past, must order the destruction of his ship and the deaths of the survivors, actions which are needless in the forward-looking model of combat followed by Kirk. Such blindness to the future is symbolically represented by the Romulan helmets, which obscure the individual's upper face, the seat of intelligence, and by positioning the crew around a windowless central pillar to suggest closure to the outside world. Even so the commander seems to regret being bound by the Romulan way as much as Kirk regrets being unable to save a wily and honorable, almost fatherly, enemy. Thus the conflict centers on the age relation between younger and older men, both positive on the moral scale despite their different loyalties.

The single episode in which a positive older woman takes part deserves mention for its uniqueness. In *Journey to Babel* we find three poles around which the plot revolves: Spock as the younger positive male ($< + \male$), his mother Amanda as the older positive female ($> + \female$), and his father as the older positive male ($> + \male$). The relations between these characters can be visualized along the lines which connect these three corners of the cube.

Catspaw provides us with a more typical setup. Here the negative younger female, Sylvia the witch ($< - \female$), matches wits against Kirk as the younger positive male ($< + \male$). Karob, the older male, who first supports Sylvia's activities, later turns against her and thus evolves in the course of the episode from $(> - \sigma)$ to $(> + \sigma)$.

In other episodes changes along an axis become more complex. In *Miri* the children of both sexes evolve on both the age and morality axes: they move from young and good to old and evil as they pass through puberty: $(< + \varphi) \rightarrow (> - \varphi)$ and $(< + \sigma) \rightarrow (> - \sigma)$. Aging in this episode means reaching puberty. Although three hundred years are necessary to arrive at this point, the "children" die of accelerated aging soon thereafter. The glandular changes of puberty leave them vulnerable to the attack of viruses produced in local experiments to retard aging. However, on a figurative level these changes image the imbalances of first love. Childhood innocence gives way to the awakening of the *anima* in males and the *animus* in females. Evil resurfaces as destructive imbalance which consumes self and others.

The Lights of Zetar provided a clear example of Jung's four faculties distributed among key characters. Plotting out its conflicts on the cube helps clarify it from another perspective. Here we see Scott as the younger positive male $(< + \sigma)$, and we hear about Mira Romaine's father, a former Star Fleet chief engineer, as the older positive male $(> + \sigma)$. The Zetars are negative male presences which are more than a thousand years old and hence possess a certain timelessness due to their independence from any body $(\lesssim - \sigma)$. Mira is the female who moves from good to evil when possessed by the Zetars and in so doing tends to incorporate their all-encompassing age: $(< + \varphi) \rightarrow (\lesssim - \varphi)$.

In *The Lights of Zetar* we have an unusually complete elaboration of the masculine principle. The Zetars as evil are balanced and eventually overcome by the forces of the positive masculine in the figure of Scott as an individual who also reincarnates characteristics of Mira's own father, also a Star Fleet engineer. Not only does a common profession relate Scott to Mira's father, but Scott's attitude toward her is consistently fatherly and protective. In addition, although Scott occupies an important position because of his special love for Mira, he is surrounded and reinforced by all of the *Enterprise* crew members who function in this episode.

Mira herself moves from a positive young female individual to self-obliteration under domination of the Zetars. Mira as embodiment of their negative force functions as if she were the pure maternal vessel, simply an unconscious maternal bearer of others. The mother, who could support the daughter's existence and serve as background for her individual consciousness, goes unmentioned as usual, leaving inactive her point of the cube $(> + ♀)$. Nonetheless Mira does emerge through the mediation of Scott, Kirk, McCoy, and Spock as a functioning individual female. The drama evolves between the planes of good and evil along the axis of gender especially focused around the relationship between Scott and Mira. Thus Mira's evolution could be plotted as $(< + ♀) \rightarrow (\lessgtr - ♀) \rightarrow (< + ♀)$.

Mira Romaine moves between good and evil as she falls into and is recovered from domination of the negative *animus*, the masculine as it possesses the female, emanating from those places beyond the familiar and conscious world of human habitation. In this way she recalls the character Elizabeth Dehner who in *Where No Man Has Gone Before* is voluntarily possessed by Gary Mitchell, as he acquires superhuman psionic powers. Moving beyond the boundaries of the galaxy activated these powers; similarly, the Zetars, remnants of a civilization which destroyed itself long ago, exist in a realm of pure psyche beyond our ken. As the ageless Zetars combine with the body of Mira Romaine, thereby blurring the differentiation between age and youth, so Gary Mitchell when he has acquired his psychic powers becomes godlike. He acquires graying hair and other characteristics usually associated with age, with the figure of the omnipotent Old Man. Thus in terms of the cube we can plot out $(< + \female) \rightarrow (< - \female) \rightarrow (< + \female)$ as Elizabeth moves into *animus* possession and recovers under Kirk's influence. Gary Mitchell however moves in only one direction: $(< + \male) \rightarrow (< - \male)$. Gary Mitchell and the Zetars share power and the disrespect for the integrity of other existing life forms which marks every manifestation of evil in *Star Trek*. From the omnivorous mothers who see life as undifferentiated dinner to the evil angel in *And the Children Shall Lead* and the spirit of Jack the Ripper in *Wolf in the Fold,* all evil figures assume that other life forms should be sacrificed for their own continuation. Although subject to gender differentiation, such forces often blur the distinction between age and youth, since evil as a force is timeless and hence has the power to override distinctions often used to separate the young from the old.

Prepare to Leave Orbit

In addition to helping visualize the structure of an episode, the cube permits us to see the dominant tendencies of the episodes taken as a whole. Even without placing each episode on the cube and statistically analyzing the results, we can begin to grasp the magnitude of the imbalances present in the series. Here perhaps emerges another use of the cube: by presenting a geometrically symmetrical image of all possible combinations, it draws our attention to those which are rarely or never used as axes for dramatic situations in *Star Trek*.

The male axis representing the older positive man/younger positive man: $(> + \male)/(< + \male)$ is dominant. In short, Kirk has many father figures from which consciously to differentiate himself. Positive younger females, however, rarely have similar opportunities. Only in *Amok Time* do we find T'Pau and T'Pring, the $(> + \female)$ and $(< + \female)$ pair; here, however, the daughter-figure does not differentiate herself from the mother-figure as Kirk does with his father-figures. On the contrary, the two are united by tradition. In *The Menagerie* the three Talosians $(> + \female)$ assume a maternal relationship to Vina $(< + \female)$, though once again the latter does not distinguish herself from the older women through emerging consciousness. Here they remain united by illusion rather than tradition.

Whereas Kirk has encountered positive father-figures such as the wizard in *Shore Leave*, who is overtly supportive of the rest and recreation necessary to the fruitful functioning of the individual, no woman in *Star Trek* has a similar advantage. Where a woman, like Odona in *The Mark of Gideon*, has a father, she is a function of his will and can easily be sacrificed to his ends. Where a woman does not have a visible father, as in the cases of Elizabeth Dehner (*Where No Man Has Gone Before*) or Edith Keeler (*The City on the Edge of Forever*), she is once again the one who must be sacrificed for the ends of the *Enterprise*. When the woman miraculously survives, as is the case with Mira Romaine, she depends upon the positive masculine for the support necessary to continue to live and grow into an individual and conscious female. There is no positive feminine principle from which to derive support for her personal and conscious existence. She does not have the option Kirk did in *The Corbomite Manoeuver* of coping with the elder male in order to identify with the positive male youth. Although the other male usually represents the principle of consciousness as predefined intellectually according to a social code, it is the son differentiating himself from such figures who embodies consciousness as a growing and changing reality. A comparable differentiation on the part of a young woman is impossible in *Star Trek* for lack of scripts that offer appropriate encounters, though this lack simply reflects a long-standing imbalance in our culture.

There are many precedents for downgrading

the opportunities, psychic as well as social, open to women. As we already mentioned, the oldest and perhaps the deepest are the many religious myths that blame the fall of humankind on women. The Fall in the Judeo-Christian tradition and elsewhere is traditionally the responsibility of a female: Eve, having had social intercourse with the snake, a creature with overtones of sexuality, eats the apple of self-awareness and invites Adam to disobey. Similarly, Jahi in the Zoroastrian tradition awakens through menstruation the sleeping powers of discord, hence of individuation and awakening self-consciousness. In India, Maya-Shakti "ate, tempted her consort to eat and was herself the apple."[3] These temptresses, by separating themselves from the Edenic goodness of preconsciousness, are blamed for making us fall. They seem like avatars of a primeval Dark Mother who weighs down humanity as surely as the force of gravity does. However, once consciousness can begin to penetrate even these obscurities, the spell can be broken, and the sexes can move toward realizing true equality of gender within both the social world and the private psychic world of each individual.

Spock as the half-alien and the archetypically masculine represents, as we have seen, areas of the imagination considered inaccessible to normal humans. He reaches out to contact an unknown which frequently embodies elements of the Negative Feminine, the obscure mother as Devil in the Dark or the omnivorous amoebic

3. Wolfgang Lederer, *The Fear of Women*, p. 137.

mother. Spock as a mediator fulfills perfectly the function of an archetype through whom the light of our consciousnesses can extend into what has previously been considered opaquely feminine.

Despite Spock's hints of a fuller future for both men and women, *Star Trek* dominantly emphasizes the masculine axis. Perhaps this orientation simply reiterates the Christian cosmic drama in which the crucial relation is between father and son.

Although the tradition of masculine dominance has a long history, there have been movements within it toward a more balanced perspective. Alchemy, condemned by the church as work of the devil, experimented not only with metals but with the marriage of minds as well. Gold was not the only alchemical image for the desired spiritual state of wholeness: the union of opposites was also symbolized by the marriage of opposites, the *coniunctio* or *chymical marriage*. Here the union of opposites is symbolized in the union of the sexes. Such concrete representations, like the Jungian diagrams of the four faculties, or the space cube, falsify human realities by pointing to a finished state.

An analogy with crystal formation might once again be useful. Although the crystal itself is a very solid structure, the process of its formation is an activity which takes place along unseen but geometrically regular axes. The poles and their axes are mathematical abstractions which nonetheless inform actual crystals. For example, the crystalline form of gold is technically labeled isometric: it has three axes of equal length which intersect at right angles. In other words it forms a cube. Thus the world of nature unexpectedly intersects with the world of ideas, for gold symbolizes the goal of alchemy and reveals a structure as balanced in three-dimensional terms as the androgyne is in two dimensions.

The chymical marriage offers a perspective in which women as well as men could relate to each other as equals. The ideal of gender equality needs to be explored in terms of its potential for providing equal access to the poles of morality and age. By viewing the world of *Star Trek* in terms of the cube, we can better appreciate the imbalance which surfaces above all in terms of gender and which Spock begins to redress.

Motion is crucial to the *Enterprise*, but not the directionless pursuit we see trapping Lokai and Bele in *Let That Be Your Last Battlefield*. The movement of the *Enterprise* on its trajectory into outer space signifies independence and true mastery of self. Similarly, *Star Trek* sets up a momentum primarily by means of Spock, who begins to restore internal gender imbalances and then to establish a special relationship with women and the rejected feminine. He tends to move the world of *Star Trek* and of our minds toward a sexual balance within which there will be no dimension so negative as to be totally in the dark. Thanks to this momentum it might become easier to imagine a world in which the masculine and the feminine will be balanced in a way analogous to the alchemical androgyne, the symmetrical cubic crystal of gold. Then we may be able to move into psychic space on a luminous trajectory like that of the *Enterprise*, freed from repetitive orbit. Once into the world of space there is no up or down—no falling but only flying.

Index of Episodes